SOMEONE'S ALWAYS LYING

BOOK ONE: BODY COUNT

S.A. WARREN

How well do you really know the people around you?
Odds are, someone's always lying.

Chapter 1
THE SETUP

The body count was high, way too high for one night and one murderer. The police officers began interviewing those still alive but seemed to be coming up with more questions than answers. What the hell happened in that house? How could a simple Birthday party turn so tragic so quickly? Well, to answer that question, we will need to go back to where it all began, a pristine house on the coveted Cul-de-sac, Manor Court, in Suburban Toronto.

It was a lovely spring morning in Toronto. The birds were chirping, the dogs were barking, and children were playing happily outside. It was a perfect day, at least weather-wise, but everything can change in an instant.

In the west end of Toronto, there is a gorgeous street called Manor Court. Every house on Manor Court is huge and spectacular; there was a reason it was one of the most sought-after addresses in all of Toronto. The funny thing is, almost every house on Manor Court looked identical. They all have the same four evergreen trees out front, long interlocking stone driveways, black roofs, doors and windows and two Lexuses parked in the driveway. If you didn't know better, you would think there was a design rule that needed to be followed, but there was one house on the street that broke all of those rules.

That house belonged to Amy and Derek Sumner. In any other neighbourhood, their home would be seen as gorgeous, but on this street, it looked like it was trying to be a slap in the face to the neighbours, and maybe it was. With a poured concrete driveway, no trees out front and grey, all the places the others were black, the house really stood out. Not to mention the Mercedes in the driveway breaking the two Lexus rule.

As a warm spring breeze blew down the street, it carried with it some very loud music, music that didn't match the contemporary look of the Sumner's home. The music felt very out of place for the neighbourhood, just like the Sumners. You see, Amy and Derek Sumner were getting ready for a themed weekend away for Amy's 35th Birthday. A weekend they hoped would be a positive reset for their momentarily rocky relationship. Unfortunately, little did they know that neither of them would make it out of the weekend alive.

Derek Sumner was just finishing getting dressed in his 70s ensemble, complete with green bell bottoms and a fitted orange and green striped shirt that looked like it should have been an old wallpaper pattern, and probably was. He was a good-looking guy, tall and lean, with short black hair and a great smile. He took one last look at himself in the mirror; he was ready to go.

"Aim, you ready yet?" Derek called to Amy from outside of the bathroom. "We're gonna be late."

"It's our party; they can't start without us." Replied Amy from inside the bathroom, where she was putting on bright red lipstick. "I'm almost ready."

Amy, of course, had pulled out all the stops to look like she had jumped straight out of the 1970s and into 2023. Amy's long blond hair was straightened perfectly, and her pink and yellow dress was barely long enough to cover her butt; she was the 1970s personified.

With an eye roll, Derek turned up the Disco music in an attempt to annoy Amy out of the bathroom. The move worked to annoy her but didn't work to hurry her up.

"Can you turn it down, please?" Amy yelled at Derek from inside the bathroom.

"What?" Derek yelled back, not turning down the music.

"Turn it down!" Amy screamed, now beyond frustrated.

"All right, all right. Keep your shirt on. I was just trying to get us in the mood for the party. You're the one who picked the theme." Derek turned the music off and left the bedroom, slamming the door behind him.

"Thanks," Amy called in reply, totally oblivious to Derek's frustration.

Buzzzz Amy picked up her phone to see a message 'Happy 35th Bday Babe! Can't wait to see you soon'. Amy smiled at the phone and put it back down, then continued examining herself in the mirror. Ding Ding, Ding Ding, Amy looked at her phone to see it was her alarm, time to leave.

Amy silenced her phone and plunked herself down on the toilet. There was one thing she had to do before she could start her weekend. Amy reached over and grabbed the pregnancy test she had left on the back of the toilet, took a deep breath and looked at the results. Negative. Again. No baby.

With an audible sigh, Amy chucked the test in the trash, took a deep breath and left the bathroom. Time to party.

Amy headed downstairs and towards the front door. Of course, the front hall was spotless, thanks to Derek and his obsession with putting everything away. This, of course, meant that Amy couldn't find anything she was looking for.

"Dare, where'd you go? Have you seen my purse and my high boots?" Amy called to Derek while searching frantically in the front hall closet.

"Ya, I grabbed them already; they're by the garage door," Derek called from the hallway that led to the garage. "Let's goooooo."

Amy made her way to the hallway where Derek was waiting and showed off her ensemble with a twirl. "So, what do you think? Do I look like I stepped straight out of Gogo cage?" Amy said, blowing Derek a kiss.

"You look awesome, Babe. What do you think of my look?" Derek modelled his outfit with a muscle flex and a wink.

"As hot as ever! Shall we?" Amy said, making her way past Derek towards the door.

As she sat to put her boots on, Derek sat beside her, suddenly acting very serious. "Are you sure about this? No one would blame you for cancelling." He said, putting a hand on her leg.

"Yeah, I'm sure. Celebrating with my friends is the best way to get my mind off things." Amy said as she finished putting on her boots and grabbed her purse.

"But a murder mystery, it's a little…."

"I'm fine. Honestly. Let's go." Amy grabbed Derek's phone from him and turned the Disco up full blast as the two of them headed out of their house for the very last time.

Derek opened the garage door and could practically feel the neighbours'; eyes on them. "Turn it down; the neighbours are gonna hate us," Derek said, getting into the car.

"Going to? They already do." Amy said, laughing as she opened the door. She took a moment to look around the neighbourhood and blow kisses to any of the neighbours that happened to be looking her way before getting in and shutting the door.

"Was that really necessary? I thought we were going to try a little harder not to piss the neighbours off." Derek said, starting the car.

"Think of it as their birthday gift to me," Amy said with a dramatic hair flip.

Derek rolled his eyes and plugged his phone into the car sending the disco music blaring through the car speakers. Amy started searching for different music to listen to when Derek took the phone out of her hand. "No way; from now on, it's all 70s all the time." Amy gave Derek 'the look' and rolled her eyes.

"Hey, it was your idea for a 70s-themed party; I'm just getting into character." And with that, Derek pulled out of the driveway, and they were off, ready to party like it was 1974.

The drive was long and slow. The house Amy had booked was in the middle of nowhere, about two hours from where they lived. Derek still couldn't understand why Amy was so insistent on having her party at this house so far away from everyone, but after what she'd been through, he wasn't going to give her a hard time. She deserved to have some fun. As they drove along, it seemed like Google maps was telling them to turn every 2 minutes; there was literally no way they could have found this place without GPS.

"Where is this place?" Derek asked as he made yet another turn.

"I don't know. It's wherever the GPS sends us. I picked it for its look, not its location." Amy said, brushing off Derek's question. "Besides, we're almost there; according to the map, we're like 10 minutes away."

No sooner had Amy commented on how close they were when the time went from 10 minutes to 20 minutes. "What, what just happened? Did you make a wrong turn or something?" Amy asked, frustrated.

"I've only turned when it tells me to. And it's not redirecting us; the time just went up for literally no reason." Derek said, looking at Amy, equally frustrated. Suddenly Amy realized why the time had jumped by 10 minutes; there was a huge tree blocking the road.

"Thing! Thing! Thing! Stop!" Amy yelled, pumping the imaginary break on her side of the car. Derek looked up just in time to see what she was talking about and slammed on the brakes.

"Where the hell did that come from? And how could the GPS possibly know that was there?" Derek said while trying to catch his breath.

"Someone must have just come through here and reported it; that's weird," Amy said, looking at the GPS that showed an accident on the road in front of them.

"Do you think we can move it?" Amy asked Derek as the two of them got out to look at the tree.

"Maybe. We should probably try; everyone is going to come this way and run into the same issue.

The tree was heavy, but with some grunting and groaning, they managed to push it just far enough off the road so they could drive past and continue on their way. Amy and Derek got back in the car and very carefully maneuvered around the tree. As soon as they got past it, the GPS went back down to 10 minutes, back on track.

Finally, after what felt like a lifetime but was more like one hour and fifty-two minutes, they heard the words, 'you've arrived at your destination. Your route guidance is complete'. The only problem was that they hadn't arrived anywhere. Derek pulled the car over and put it into park while Amy looked up the address on her phone, mildly freaking out that she'd put the wrong address.

"I don't get it; this is the right address; we should be here." Amy had more than a bit of panic in her voice, and Derek could sense it.

"How about I just keep driving a bit, and we'll see if we come to it? Maybe the directions aren't that precise in the middle of nowhere.

Derek slowly began driving, and it wasn't a minute later that they came across a long driveway barely noticeable from the main road. Derek turned down the driveway and followed it up the winding road until they got to a gate. A locked gate. "Shit. Now what?" Derek said, full of frustration.

"This must be the place!" Amy jumped out of the car, phone in hand and walked over to the gate. She opened up a small box with a pin pad inside and scrolled through her messages until she found one from someone named Courtney. 'Can't wait to have you guys. The code for the gate is 89483756'. Amy punched the code in and waited for a moment before the gate slowly started to open before getting back into the car and heading inside.

They passed through the gate and continued on the long and winding road. Derek noticed in the rearview mirror that the gate was still open behind them, but the fence on either side stretched as far as he could see. What is this place? He thought to himself as he continued up the never-ending driveway.

Suddenly a huge house appeared in the distance; it had to be at least 10,000 square feet. Derek pulled up to the front entrance to the house, if you could even call it a house, and the two of them got out of the car. The house was more like a sprawling mansion with what looked like about 20 rooms inside. It certainly wasn't new, but it wasn't that old, either. In fact, it looked like it was built sometime in the 1970s.

"What is this place? Where did you find it?" Derek said to Amy as they made their way to the front door, Derek turned to lock the car, and he noticed the gate was closed behind them. They rang the doorbell and then waited for a moment.

"What did this place cost us?" Derek asked Amy in shock. Before Amy could answer, the door opened, and they were greeted by a very young, very perky Courtney and her chihuahua, Mango.

"Hiya! You must be Amy and Derek, welcome!" Courtney opened the door widely to let Amy and Derek inside. As they walked through the front door, Courtney's phone buzzed; she took it out of her pocket, looked at the message and giggled to herself, sent a quick reply then put it back away to give her attention back to her guests. Courtney's house was unreal. It was literally like they stepped back in time to the 1970s.

"I told ya, it's like being in the 70s, isn't it wild?" Courtney asked with a giggle.

"This is your house?" Derek asked Courtney incredulously; none of this was making sense to him.

"Yes, but no. This is my parents' house, so like I live here, but it isn't my house. They're in Italy for the month, so I'm renting it out on weekends to make some extra money." Courtney said, putting Mango down to let her run. "Looks like the tour guide is ready to show you around, shall we?" Courtney said, following Mango. Derek gave Amy a WTF look, and she just blew him a kiss. Now, to see the mansion.

Chapter 2
THE MANSION

Courtney led the way down the main hallway, following Mango all the way to the back of the house as Derek and Amy trailed behind.

"This is the main hallway; it goes down the center of the house; those are the stairs to upstairs," Courtney said, pointing to a large spiral staircase in the middle of the house.

Once they got to the back of the house, Courtney stopped and turned to face her guests. "To the right is the family room; it's the largest sitting room in the house," Courtney said, entering the room with Derek and Amy close behind her.

"There is enough seating in this room for all of your guests, and the fireplace works in case you need it." Courtney said, stepping to the side so Derek and Amy could better see the room.

The family room was indeed massive, with a large red leather sectional sofa and six separate chairs that looked incredibly comfortable. The centre of the room had a circular carpet and a very elaborate chandelier hanging from the ceiling. It was like the ultimate '70s sitting room came to life.

Once Amy and Derek had had a chance to look around for a minute or two, Courtney continued on her tour. "Ok, the next room along this side of the hall is the library," Courtney said, going into the next room, which couldn't have been mistaken for anything other than a library. Three of the four walls in the room were covered with bookshelves filled to the ceiling with books.

This room also had a fireplace and eight chairs around a coffee table. Perfect for curling up with a good book but probably not the ideal spot for a party.

"Wow, this room is gorgeous, but I don't think we will spend much time in here this weekend, looks like a cozy spot to relax, though," Amy said as she picked a book off the shelf.

"Agreed, this certainly isn't a great party room, but I want to make sure you have the whole layout. It can get a bit confusing with all of the doors," Courtney said, leaving the library and heading to the next room.

"Ok, this is the parlour, it's the smallest room, but it's a good spot to wait for your guests to arrive as it has the best view of the driveway," Courtney said, showing them the little room at the front of the house. The parlour was small compared to the other rooms but large compared to anyone else's house. It had two dark green sofas, a bar cart, and a large coffee table. It was also fully carpeted with long shag carpet; it looked like it was right out of the 70s, like everywhere else in the house.

Courtney left the parlour and made her way past the front door to the other side of the house. "This is the living room, and it's the only room in the house with a TV," Courtney said, leading the way into the large room across from the parlour.

"Where?" Derek asked, looking around the room that had three black leather sofas and lots of tables but no TV in sight.

Courtney picked up a remote from the coffee table and pushed a button. Instantly the wall opened, and a massive flat-screen TV appeared. "Wow, that's not very 70s!" Amy said with shock.

"It sure isn't. The 70's stuff is totally for effect; the house has all of the modern conveniences; it just looks retro." Courtney said, pushing the same button, so the TV disappeared again.

"Follow me." Courtney left the living room and made her way into the next room, the dining room. "So this is the dining room. As you can see, the table is set just how you requested." Courtney said, showing off the beautifully set table in the centre of the massive room.

"Looks great. Thanks so much!" Amy said, examining the red tablecloth.

"My pleasure! You certainly made it worth my while." Courtney said with a smile.

Derek shot Amy a look, worth her while could only mean one thing, Amy paid a fortune for this night. Amy caught Derek's gaze, and all she could do was wink and blow him a kiss. No point in getting into it at this point.

"Ok, so the last room on this floor is the kitchen." Courtney led Amy and Derek down the adjoining hallway into the kitchen, which was absolutely full of food.

"Anything that is room temperature is on the counter, anything cold is in one of the fridges, and anything that needs to be served hot is in an oven warming." Courtney stepped aside so Amy and Derek could survey the kitchen. It was huge.

The Kitchen had three fridges, two ovens and more counter space than they had ever seen. There was also a door to the backyard that they looked through. "The backyard is amazing!" Amy said, looking outside at the pool, tennis court and gazebos.
"Ya, it's probably my fave thing about this house," Courtney said with a smile. "You're welcome to use it if you want."

"Ok, so that finishes the downstairs. Should we head up?" Courtney led Amy and Derek out of the kitchen and up the winding staircase to the upstairs.

"Oh, if you want the WIFI it's 452 Walker; password is Mango1 with a capital M," Courtney said as Derek and Amy both pulled out their phones.

"Here is the upstairs; there are nine bedrooms total. Four on the left and five on the right, the bedroom above the kitchen is the primary bedroom which I assume you will use as your own if you want to put your bags in there. Also, the last two bedrooms on the right had two single beds instead of a queen, in case anyone prefers that. " Courtney said, opening the door to the large bedroom at the back of the house.

"Each bedroom also has an en suite, and I forgot to show you, but there are also two washrooms on the main floor. One off of the family room and one between the living room and dining room." Courtney said to Amy and Derek, who were no longer listening as they were too busy being in awe of the bedroom before them.

"Is there a basement?" Amy asked as Derek went downstairs to grab the luggage from the car.

"Yes, the basement stairs are at the back of the house, off the kitchen. There is a billiard room, large sitting room, laundry room, bar and bathroom down there. Feel free to use it if you'd like, but it isn't 70s themed; it's very modern and doesn't really fit with your theme." Courtney said as she and Amy waited for Derek to return.

"Oh, ok. Thanks for the heads up; we probably won't go down there. I was just curious." Amy headed into the large en suite and almost fell over. It was incredible and almost as big as her entire bedroom at home. "Wow, just wow." She said as she looked inside of the sauna.

Derek returned with the bags as Amy and Courtney looked through the washroom. "Ok, that's everything." He said, putting their stuff down on the floor. Derek took a seat on the bed, and the moment he sat down, the doorbell rang.

"Oh, sounds like your guests are arriving. Is there anything else you need from me?" Courtney asked as the three headed down the stairs. Derek and Amy looked at each other.

"No, I think we're good. Thanks!" Amy said as they headed towards the front door.

"Ok, great! You know how to reach me if you need me. Mango! Mango!" Courtney started putting her coat on as she called out to Mango, who had been conspicuously missing since the tour began. "Mango!" Just as Courtney was about to go searching for her pup, he came bounding down the hall with a little squeaker toy in his mouth. "Come on you." She said, picking up Mango as he squeaked away on his toy.

Courtney opened the front door revealing Layla and Raegan, who were standing outside waiting to be let in. "Hello and goodbye, ladies! Have fun tonight." Courtney said as she headed towards her car.

"Thanks, nice to meet you!" Layla called to Courtney as she left.

"Layla! Raegan! OMG, I'm so excited you're here, come in, come in!" Amy hugged her two friends as they stepped into the front hall.

"Wow, look at this place! It must have cost you a fortune!" Raegan said as she took off her coat.

"Just a small one." Amy joked as Derek took the coats and hung them up in the closet.

Layla was shorter than Amy, with short blonde hair and glasses. She was dressed in orange bell-bottom jeans and a blue and orange blouse with a huge collar. Raegan was a lot taller than Layla, with shoulder-length black hair and piercing green eyes. She had on an ankle-length red skirt and a red-and-white striped blouse that really accentuated her height.

"So, how do we look?" Layla said, spinning to show off her outfit.

"You both look amazing, love, love, love it!" Amy said, giving Layla a big hug.

"Shall we get a drink?" Amy asked, grabbing Layla's hand and pulling her towards the kitchen.

"Is there somewhere we can put our bag?" Raegan asked, picking the bag up from in front of the door.

"Yes, you can take bedroom number one, the front room on the left. Then meet us in the kitchen when you're done." Amy said, pointing up the stairs. Raegan started up the stairs as Derek, Layla and Amy headed to the kitchen to get some drinks.

They hadn't made it ten steps before the doorbell rang again. Derek stopped and turned around, "I'll get it."

As Layla and Amy made their way to the kitchen, Derek went to the front door to see who was there. When he opened the door, he was met by Jack, Kara, Brook and Bryce.

Jack, who was in his early 30s, was the first through the door. He was shorter than Derek and a little geeky looking with a bad haircut and clothes that didn't quite fit. He had on brown corduroy bell bottoms that were too short and an ugly silk shirt with yellow anchors on it for some reason.

"Hi, I'm Derek, and you are?" Derek asked, extending a hand to greet Jack.
"Nice to meet you; I'm Jack. Kara and I work with Amy." Jack said, stepping aside to introduce Kara.

Kara waved hello nervously as she entered the hall. She was thin, incredibly thin, with curly brown hair and brown eyes. She had on a bright green and yellow dress that looked like it should be fitted but was hanging off of her like it was five sizes too big.

"Hey Derek, we've heard lots about you from…." Kara hadn't even gotten her sentence out before Brook pushed past her and wrapped her arms around Derek.

"Derek! How's life? It's been so long! Too long!" Brook gave Derek a huge kiss on the cheek, leaving a perfect lipstick mark on his face.

If you were wondering who the party girl in the group was, hands down it was Brook. She was known for being boisterous, loud and loving to be the centre of attention. Brook also never shies away from a challenge, and when Amy told her to dress for the 70s, she dressed for the 70s. Brook had on a vintage skirt and shirt combo that was gorgeous. It had brown and orange stripes and a matching headband that fit perfectly into her straight black hair. She also had on massive orange sunglasses that she clearly couldn't see out of, but she was committed to her look.

Derek finished hugging Brook hello and managed to peel her off of him just in time to say hello to Bryce. "Bryce! How are ya! It's been a while!" Derek said, putting out his hand to shake Bryce's.

Bryce offered Derek a fist bump instead, "Sup?" He said as Derek bumped his fist hello. Bryce was your stereotypical bodybuilder with muscles bursting out of his clothes that he probably bought two sizes too small on purpose. Bryce isn't really one for participating, so it was clear that Brook was responsible for his perfect 70s attire. Bryce had on skinny jeans that were a little skinnier than they needed to be and a tight black shirt that was only buttoned halfway up.

"Amy, Layla and Raegan are in the kitchen getting drinks if you want to head that way to join them. You can also take your bags upstairs and snag yourselves a bedroom. Any room with a door open is fine." Derek said, moving to the side to let them pass.

Kara pulled Derek over to the side, "do any of the rooms have single beds?" she asked, trying not to let Jack see what she was asking.

"Yes, the last two bedrooms on the right both have two single beds," Derek replied quietly. Kara mouthed the word thanks then grabbed her bag and headed upstairs.

Brook and Bryce took bedroom number two on the left side, right beside Layla and Raegan and Jack and Kara took number nine at the back of the house, where Kara could ensure they had single beds.

Once the four of them had put their bags down, they made their way to the kitchen to join Amy, Raegan and Layla and to make themselves a drink.

"B-day girrrrrrl! Are you ready to party?" Brook said, making quite the entrance into the kitchen.

"Brookey! Get over here, girl!" Amy put down her drink and gave Brook a huge hug and kiss on the cheek. "You know my friends Raegan and Layla, right?" Amy said as Brook, Layla and Raegan got reacquainted.

"Hey, Amy, happy birthday!" Amy turned around to see Jack and Kara standing in the doorway together but not together, if you know what I mean.

"Hey, guys! So glad you could come! Make sure to grab yourselves a drink; we have literally everything!" Amy put an arm around Kara and Jack and led them over to the drinks; they grabbed themselves a wine cooler and a beer.

Amy turned around to see Derek and Bryce standing in the doorway; they seemed to be chatting quietly; then Bryce laughed and shoved Derek hard enough to push him into the doorframe.

"Sorry, man, sometimes I forget my own strength," Bryce said with a laugh.

"No worries, I get it," Derek replied as he rubbed his shoulder.

"Bryce-Bryce! Why don't you have a drink in your hand? Get over here!" Amy motioned for Bryce to come over, which he excitedly did; he was ready for a drink.

Derek felt a little neglected but decided to suck it up and grab a beer. "So, what'd this set ya back?" Bryce asked Derek while taking a sip of his rum and coke.

"I have no idea; you'll have to ask Amy. But don't tell me what she says; I'm gonna need a few more drinks in me before I'm crossing that bridge." Bryce and Derek shared a laugh, then decided to take their drinks into the family room and sit down.

"So Aim, how are you doing? Like, really, how are you doing?" Layla asked, pulling Amy aside. This was the first time she had to address the elephant in the room that night, but she knew it wouldn't be the last.

"I'm ok. I mean, it's been a hard few months, but it's starting to get better. I'm glad to have all of my friends here tonight to help me let loose!" Amy replied with a forced smile, all while picturing her parents' fatal car accident in her mind. She shook her head to try and rid her mind of the image and took a shot of vodka to numb the pain.

Amy forced a smile, and Layla decided to change the subject. Unfortunately, she picked an even worse subject. "Any news on the…." Layla mimed a baby bump and immediately regretted it. Amy glared at her and took yet another shot telling her everything she needed to know.

"Come here, you crazy bitch I've missed you so much!" Brook was back again, hugging Amy so hard she almost knocked her right off her feet and managed to knock her right into Jack spilling his drink all over the floor.

"Awe shit, sorry," Brook said, making no effort to clean up the mess.

"It's ok. These things happen," Jack replied as he grabbed a dishcloth to clean the floor.

"Why don't we head into the family room?" Kara said, getting Jack a fresh drink.

Jack, Kara, Amy, Brook, Layla and Raegan all grabbed their drinks and made their way into the family room. "How long have you known Amy?" Kara asked Layla, making small talk.

"Since we were 5!" Amy said, interrupting.

"What she said, but it was actually like four and a half," Layla replied with a playful smile.

"How about you?" Kara said to Brook, who was somehow already drunk.

"Amy and I met in college, and we are besties for life, right Aim?" Brook said, holding her drink up in the air.

"You know it, girlfriend!" Amy replied, blowing Brook a kiss and making Layla feel a little uncomfortable and a little left out.

Ding dong. "Derek, can you get that?" Amy said as she sat down in the very centre of the massive sectional couch. Derek put his drink down and headed to the front door to meet the next group to arrive.

Derek opened the front door to another large group of friends. The first one through the door was Amy's cousin, Claire.

"Claire, good to see you. So glad you could make it." Derek said, taking Claire's coat. Claire was a little younger than Amy and twice as bubbly, all she had to do was smile at you, and you would immediately feel warm and safe. Claire had short red hair, green eyes and freckles, and she was dressed in bell-bottom jeans and a crop top with ruffles.

"So good to see you too! This is Mick, my new boyfriend," Claire motioned to introduce Mick, who silently entered the house and nodded his head hello. Mick was quite a bit older than Claire, probably late 30s and had a buzzcut and a permanent grimace. He was also the least-themed person so far tonight. He was wearing jeans and a t-shirt, clearly just his regular clothes.

"Hi, Mick, nice to meet you. If you want to take your bags upstairs, you can take any bedroom with an open door." Derek said, taking Mick's coat. Mick nodded in thanks, grabbed the bag and headed upstairs.

Derek gave Claire a, 'really, him?' look, and she just smiled back. "Drinks are in the kitchen, and everyone is in the family room; head to the back of the house," Derek said as Claire made her way to grab a drink and find the others.

The next through the door were Anders and Lin. Anders and Lin had been couple friends of Amy and Derek's for a while, and Lin was clearly ready to party. "Lin, Anders! So good to see you guys!" Derek said, taking their coats and hanging them in the closet. "You too, we haven't seen you since the funer…" the moment the words left Anders' mouth, he immediately regretted it.

Lin worked fast to change the subject. "This place is intense! I can see Amy went all out for her birthday as always." Lin and Amy had been friends since high school, and Lin knew her party style well.

Lin was dressed in a burnt orange pantsuit with a black frill blouse underneath. Her dark hair was straightened and almost made it down to her shoulders, but not quite. Lin was naturally beautiful, and even though she never wore makeup, she always looked like she had mascara on; Amy would never admit it, but she was eternally envious of her effortless good looks.

Anders, on the other hand, was just your average everyday guy. He was medium height, medium build, with brown hair and brown eyes. Anders was known for always being the voice of reason, and he took that role very seriously. Anders was dressed in jeans and a t-shirt, and although he was probably wearing one of his everyday outfits, it perfectly fit the 70s theme.

"Head upstairs and grab any room with an open door. Then you can find Amy and everyone else in the family room at the back of the house." Derek said as he finally got around to welcoming Colleen and Marco.

"Hey guys, thanks for hanging up your own coats. It's so tough when everyone arrives all at once." Derek was starting to feel a little exasperated being the one and only member of the welcoming committee.

"Don't worry! You just need to make sure you keep your Chakras in order, ya know what I mean? I brought some essential oils with me; we should definitely get those on, clear out some of that stale air," Colleen was one of Amy's closest friends, but she was also a notorious MLM hun and tended to drive everyone nuts with her constant need to sell some of the most ridiculous products. Her current venture was essential oils, but before that, she tried selling shampoo, makeup, and cleaning products.

Colleen was dressed for the occasion in a dress so loud and colourful that it probably would have glowed in the dark. Marco, on the other hand, was wearing the drabbest brown suit possible; if he decided to lay down on the wood floor, he probably would have blended right in, and to be honest, he looked just about ready to do that.

Colleen and Marco had been dating forever, but they had never been engaged and showed no sign of ever getting married. This clearly drove Colleen nuts, but Marco seemed to be stuck between a rock and a hard place, not willing to commit to Colleen for life and not willing to break up with her either.

Marco grabbed their bag and headed upstairs to put it in a bedroom while Colleen and Derek headed back to join the others.

By the time Derek and Colleen made it to the kitchen, Lin, Anders, Claire and Mick had all gotten themselves a drink and were just about to head into the family room to join the party.

"Colleen, grab yourself a drink, then meet us in the family room; it's just across the hall," Derek said, leaving the kitchen.

Derek entered the family room, finally ready to sit down and relax. "So, everyone arrived all at once. Layla, Raegan, Brook, Bryce, Kara, Jack meet Claire, Colleen, Anders, Lin and Mick. Marco should be here in a minute; he's just putting the bags upstairs." Derek slumped down in his chair and grabbed his beer. He was just about to take a sip when the doorbell rang.

Derek looked at Amy. "I thought everyone was here, is someone else coming?" Derek asked, somewhat exasperated.

"Don't worry; I'll get it," Amy said, getting up and heading to the door before Derek could protest. "Wifi?" Mick said literally out of nowhere.

"Oh, uh, It's 452 Walker; password is Mango1 with a capital M." Derek replied as everyone put it into their phones.

As soon as Amy left the room, the energy died, and an awkward silence took over. Thankfully, Brook had no problem pointing it out.

"Well, this is a little awkward. Like we all know Amy and most of us have met each other in the past, but none of us are really friends. It's like we're all friends in law. It's a bit weird." Brook pointing it out, effectively broke the tension, and everyone immediately relaxed.

Suddenly the group went from a random group of strangers to instant friends. Everyone started chatting amongst themselves, and the party's vibe instantly changed. That is until Amy returned with the last two guests.

"Asher? Michelle? I didn't know you guys were coming. We haven't seen you since the… it's been a while." Derek said as he reluctantly shook Asher's hand and hugged Michelle.

Asher put his arm around Amy, "It has. I know we weren't all on the best of terms, but I decided to call Amy to wish her a happy birthday, and we got to talking. We worked things out, and she invited us to the party, last minute. I mean, I couldn't miss my baby sister's big 3-5 no matter how mad we might have been at each other." Amy and Asher shared a hug, and the party vibe returned, thankfully.

Asher was dressed in a very slick 70s business suit; he looked like someone who might have been managing a band or possibly selling drugs back in the day. Michelle, on the other hand, was looking her usual frumpy self. She had on a dress that didn't quite fit and looked like she had found it at goodwill on the way there and decided it was good enough.

Amy stood at the front of the family room and held her glass up. "Well, my friends, we are all here, and I can't thank you enough for not only driving all the way out to the middle of nowhere but also for fully embracing my 70s-themed birthday party." Amy took a big drink from her glass as everyone cheered.

"So, what do you say we kick off the murder mystery and get this party started!" Amy grabbed a black box from the side of the room and put it on the table.

"Everyone, cell phones in the box, we need to be authentic to the 1970s!" Amy threw her phone in the box and then passed it around so everyone could put their phones inside. She practically had to pry Brook's phone from her hand, but everyone's phones made it into the box. Amy locked the box and placed the key in her bra.

"All right, who's ready for dinner?" Amy asked as everyone cheered. The group left the family room and headed into the dining room; the party was finally getting started.

Chapter 3
THE DINNER

Amy was the first one in the dining room, the table was set beautifully, but there was no food to be seen. Right, they will need to serve themselves.

"Ok, totally forgot that the food is cooked but not actually being served to us, so everyone grab your plate and head into the kitchen; we'll do this buffet style." Amy put her drink down at the head of the table and grabbed her plate.

Amy walked into the kitchen to another realization. Right, the food wasn't put out for them; it needed to be taken out of the fridge and oven first. Amy put her plate down and went to grab the salads out of the fridge. Layla was next into the kitchen and immediately started to help by getting the warm dishes out of the oven.

Derek started laying the dishes out along the counter, and in just a few moments, the buffet was ready to go. "Ok, help yourselves!" Amy said, picking her plate back up and going to the back on the line.

"No way, birthday girl, you go first!" Brook said, pushing everyone to the side to let Amy pass.

Amy made her way to the front and started to fill her plate. There were so many delicious and unusual dishes to choose from that she didn't quite know where to begin. As Amy worked her way through the conga line of food, her friends began filing in behind her.

Claire was right behind Amy, and she took the opportunity to check in on her cousin, "How are you doing?" Claire said as she scooped some potatoes onto her plate.

"I'm great! How are things with you?" Amy replied, not even really listening to the question.

"I'm fine. But I mean, really, how are you? I'm still so sad about your parents. Aunt Jean and Uncle Luke were like my second parents. When I think about how much I miss them I can't imagine how you feel." Claire said, swallowing back the lump in her throat.

Amy put her plate down and hugged Claire, " Thank you. I miss them. A lot. But I'm trying to get back to living my life as best as I can. I know that's what they would have wanted. Thanks for asking." Amy picked her plate back up and gave Claire a big smile before continuing with the buffet.

Brook and Bryce were next in line, with Derek next and Marco following close behind. Anders and Kara ended up getting to the counter at the same time and had an awkward Canadian moment where each of them waited for the other to go first.

"Go ahead." Anders finally said, stepping aside to let Kara go next.

"Don't mind if I do." Lin chimed in, cutting in behind Kara and in front of Anders.

Everyone else quickly filled their plates, with Jack and Asher at the end of the line. As soon as the guests had filled their plates, they made their way into the dining room to make sure they didn't miss a moment of the party.

The friends took their seats at the table, with Derek and Amy seated at either end. To Amy's left was Brook, Bryce, Lin, Marco, Anders, Colleen and Michelle; to Amy's right it was Layla, Raegan, Kara, Jack, Claire, Mick and Asher.

As soon as everyone sat down, the volume grew to an incredible level. There were instantly six different conversations going on at once, and it was nearly impossible to keep everything straight. Amy stood up and quietly clinked her glass. Nothing. Amy cleared her throat and tried a second time; this got everyone's attention.

Silence fell across the group as Amy started to speak, "Thank you all so much for coming here tonight to help me celebrate my thirtieth birthday!" Amy held up her glass as everyone hooted and cheered.

"Thank you, thank you. As you know, the past few months have been hard since losing my parents, but all of you have been there for me and made this tough time a little more bearable." Amy paused for a moment to wipe a tear and noticed that Asher was giving her a reluctant half-smile which was more than a little surprising.

"We love you, Aim!" Brook said, blowing Amy a kiss. Amy pretended to catch it and put it on her cheek.

"Ok, it is time to forget about reality and transport ourselves back in time to the 70s. So take a deep breath and get into character." Amy took a very dramatic deep breath, as did Colleen and Kara.

Amy cleared her throat, "Thank you all for coming in such awesome costumes. I totally feel like we've gone back to the 70s."

"I can't believe people used to eat like this. The food is all so heavy." Lin said, interrupting Amy mid-thought as she took a spoonful of Jell-o mould and wobbled it on her spoon.

"I know, I know, but I wanted everything to be authentic; some of the stuff is good. Besides, it's just for one night." Amy continued getting things back on track.

"So before you arrived, you each got a card outlining who you are and whether or not you're the murderer. So start asking each other questions and see if you can get to the bottom of the mystery." Amy sat down, and everyone started to talk amongst themselves.

"So, Kara, is it?" Lin said to Kara, who was sitting across from her.

"Ya, Lin, right?" Kara replied slightly nervously. "I've been watching you; where were you last Friday night?" Lin said in an accusatory tone.

"What? What do you mean I was at home and…" Kara started to trail off, feeling very taken aback by Lin's question.

"Relax! I was just getting into the game, didn't mean to freak you out." Lin said with a laugh.

Kara laughed as well, but she was still feeling very put on the spot. "Oh, duh. I think it's this house; it's so big it's making me a little jumpy." Kara replied, trying to cover up her nervous energy.

"I know what you mean; this house is a little creepy, just something about it," Raegan added, making Kara feel better.

Suddenly Amy stood up from her chair again, "I forgot! Everyone needs to go around and introduce their characters. We can't solve the murder until we know the suspects. I'll start.." Amy cleared her throat and flicks her hair, "Hey, ya'll! I'm Margot, a T.V. star best known for starring in the soap opera Days of Disco." Amy flicked her hair one more time then sat down.

Amy looked to Brook, who stood up next, "My turn! Hi, I'm Linda, a Go-Go dancer with three kids and a heart of gold. Oh, this is fun! Bryce, your turn." Brook sat down and looked at Bryce, then poked him in the ribs to get him to stand up.

Bryce reluctantly stood up, "Hey, I'm John the Disco King." Bryce sat down as soon as he finished speaking.

"Do the move! Do the move!" Brook motioned for Bryce to get back up and do his 'Saturday Night Fever' move. Bryce rolled his eyes, stood up, did the move, and instantly sat back down as everyone cheered.

Lin was next, "Hi, I'm Melissa, the pop starrrrrrr." Lin broke into a very dramatic and very bad singing voice as all of her friends cheered her on.

Marco stood up next, "I'm Tank, the football player." Marco was quickly back in his seat, clearly unamused, but at least he was playing along.

Anders popped to his feet, "All right, looks like I'm up next. My name is Carl Van Lang, and I'm a famous inventor." Anders took a moment to bow to his friends' claps and then took a seat.

Colleen was up next, and everyone already knew how this was going to go, "Hi, I'm Olivia. Famous female entrepreneur, which is super appropriate since, in real life, I have my very own business." Colleen was probably going to elaborate, but Michelle quickly reminded her of exactly what everyone thought of her 'business.'

"Hun, you sell essential oils for an MLM. Cool your jets." Michelle said, not even attempting to soften her comment. Everyone chuckled under their breath. Michelle continued on to introduce herself, "Anyways, Hi, I'm Monica, the fashion model; make sure you get my good side." Michelle did some poses as everyone pretended to take her picture.

"All right, I'm up next." Derek said, standing up, "I'm Derek, the secret agent. Nobody saw me here tonight, got it?" Derek sat back down and immediately went back to eating.

Next up was Mick, who was really having none of this whole role-playing thing, "I'm Carlos. The pimp." Mick didn't even stand up, and from what everyone had seen of Mick so far, it wasn't surprising.

Claire, on the other hand, was much more enthusiastic, "My turn, this is fun! Hey guys, I'm Jenna, animal rights activist. Fur is Murder!" Claire pumped her fist in the air as everyone cheered before sitting back down and turning to Jack, who was up next.

Jack half stood up, "I'm Gerald, the pilot." Jack was back in his seat and taking a sip of his drink as soon as the word pilot left his mouth.

Kara remained in her seat as she introduced herself, not wanting to make Jack feel bad, "I'm Bella, Psychic Medium."

Next, it was Raegan's turn. She was so red in the face it was hard to even tell where her mouth was,

"I'm Kimberley. Porn Star." Raegan said the porn star part as quietly as possible, but it didn't stop everyone from hooting and hollering.

And last but not least, it was Layla's turn. Layla stood up to introduce herself, bringing energy back to the room, "I'm Lola, the Vegas Showgirl! Woot woot!" Layla did a quick dance before retaking her seat.

Amy stood up again and began reading from a small card she had removed from her bra. "Ok, now that we've all been formally introduced, it's time for the backstory. It was a dark and stormy night in 1974 when a group of friends got together for a dinner party thrown by the famous actor Dick Markman. The friends arrived and started enjoying dinner when the power suddenly went out. When it came back on, Dick was dead, and all of the guests were suspects. Now it's up to you to ask each other questions and discover the murderer. All right, let the games begin. Bon Appetite." Amy sat back down, and everyone continued eating and asking each other questions. The mystery party was finally getting going.

The noise volume in the room was steadily rising until it was impossible to discern any specific conversations.

"What were you doing when…."

"Tell me about your job…."

"How come you never told me…."

"Help, she's choking!" That one cut through the noise.

Raegan stood up suddenly and said it again, "Help! She's choking!" Kara had her hands on her throat and was clearly in distress.

The jumble of noise rose again, but this time everyone was focused on the same thing, "Someone help her!"

"What do we do!"

"Does anyone know what to do?" As the panic worsened, Kara started to tear up and almost lost consciousness.

As everyone stood around her panicked, Mick calmly cut through the group, walked over and in one quick motion, successfully performed the choking procedure sending Kara crumbling to the floor in relief as she gasped for air. All of the guests crowded around Kara to confirm she was ok, all except for Mick, who returned to his seat to continue his meal.

"Someone pass her a drink," Amy said while sitting beside Kara on the floor, rubbing her back.

"Here, take this," Michelle said, passing Amy a drink.

"Thanks, Michelle. Here Kara have some sips of water. Are you ok?" Amy said, helping Kara up and back to her seat.

"I think so. I'm ok now. Thanks for saving me, Mick." Kara looked to Mick with a tear in her eye; he acknowledged her with a half-smile between bites, then went right back to his dinner.

"Are you sure you're ok? That was a really close call; maybe we should call for an ambulance or take you to the hospital to be checked out." Derek said in a shaky voice.

Seeing an opportunity to get closer to Kara, Jack got up from his seat and came over to provide Kara some comfort.

"I'm fine." Kara continued sipping her water, making sure not to look at Jack. After a few moments of being ignored, he went back to his seat, feeling majorly rejected.

Everyone sat staring at their plates in silence, Mick and Marco went back to eating, and everyone else basically chased their food around their plate. After a few very long, very awkward moments, Asher decided to break the ice. "Maybe we should all get out of here; seems like the evening isn't off to a great start." No one said anything in agreement, but no one defended staying either.

"I have some essential oils and a diffuser in my bag upstairs. Maybe I can put it on and help to change the whole vibe in this place." Colleen said, getting up from her seat and excitedly running to the bedroom.

"I don't want this to ruin the night; I'm ok, honestly. I guess 70s food just isn't my thing." Kara managed a half smile and a fake laugh while everyone else laughed uncomfortably; it was so awkward.

And Colleen was about to make it more awkward. "Got my diffuser! Get ready to feel totally Zen!"

Colleen poured the leftover water from her glass into the diffuser, added some drops of essential oil, and plugged it in. She then proceeded to dramatically breathe in and out while encouraging everyone else to join her. They didn't.

While the friends worked hard to ignore Colleen, an unexpected interruption cut through the silence. Ding Dong. Everyone looked at each other surprised, then turned to Amy, who shrugged; clearly she wasn't expecting the visitor either.

"I'll get it," Jack said, popping up from his seat; he was still feeling awkward after the whole Kara shrug off and figured he would take the opportunity to get out of the room for a minute.

While everyone waited for Jack to return, they continued eating and drinking; the vibe was starting to improve a bit, maybe the essential oils were actually working. Jack returned from the door with a large purple box in his hands.

"Ohhhh, is that a present for me?" Amy said, standing up with excitement.

"Looks like it." Jack handed Amy the present, then sat back down in his seat and went back to his now ice-cold dinner.

Amy opened the card on top and read it aloud, "Happy Birthday, Amy; we are so gladto have you here; please accept this surprise as a welcome gift." She put the card down and removed the lid from the top of the box. Inside the box were 16 small gifts, each with the name of a different guest on top. "Oh, weird! Looks like it isn't a gift just for me. There's something inside for each of you.

Amy got up and walked around the table, passing out a present to each guest; the last one in the box was for her. Once Amy was seated, they each opened their gifts and were shocked.

In each box was a note folded in half; on the front of each note were the words, 'you might not want to read this aloud,' and on the inside of each note was a secret that rocked the reader to the core.

"What the hell is this? Who did this? This isn't funny." Amy said, throwing her note down on the table. Layla looked down at the empty box sitting between her and Amy and noticed there was still one more note at the bottom of the box; she picked it up and read it to the group, "You've got a secret, each of you. You'll pretend it's a lie, but you know it's true. Want to keep your secrets safe? Ignore the murders and leave this place. If you decide to stay instead, the countdown is on. You're already dead."

Layla put down the note and looked around at everyone, shocked. She then noticed a number on the back of the note that Amy had thrown on the table; it was number one. She turned her note over and saw the number fourteen on her note.

"There are numbers on the backs of all of our notes, Amy has number one, and I have number fourteen," Layla said, showing the number on her note. Everyone flipped their notes over and read out their numbers one by one.

"Two." Said, Colleen.
"Three." Said, Anders.
"Four." Said, Asher.
"Five." Said, Kara.
"Six." Said, Michelle.
"Seven." Said, Raegan.
"Eight." Said, Derek.
"Nine." Said, Lin.
"Ten." Said, Claire.
"Eleven." Said, Bryce.
"Twelve." Said, Marco.
"Thirteen." Said, Jack.
"Fifteen." Said, Brook.

"Sixteen." Said, Mick.

Everyone sat in total silence, if the party wasn't ruined before, it certainly was now. Amy was the first to break the silence, she had had enough. "What is going on? Seriously who is behind this? This is not funny!" Amy looked around to see if anyone would crack but nope. All of her friends looked as confused as she felt.

"Well, I'm out. Come on, Raegan, let's go." Layla said, standing up and putting her note in her pocket. Raegan was quick behind her. As the two left the dining room and headed to the hall, the other party guests got up and started moving around the house, unsure of what to do.

"I'll get the bag if you want to start the car," Raegan said to Layla as they got to the front door.

Marco and Claire had now caught up to Layla as the three of them grabbed their coats and stepped outside. "Why is the gate closed?" Marco said to Claire, who was standing beside him.

"It was open when we pulled up; maybe it's closed but not locked," Claire replied, hoping she was right.

Marco jogged over to the gate and tried to push it open; then he tried to pull it, no luck. It was locked. "It's locked. Who has the code for the gate?" Marco yelled to Claire and Layla as he jogged back.

"I don't have the code; it was open when we got here, too," Layla said with a shaky voice.

"So how are we supposed to open it?" Claire said, almost in tears.

Marco, Claire and Layla headed back into the house, where Raegan was standing with her bag ready to go. "What's going on? Why aren't we leaving?" Raegan asked with panic in her voice.

"The gate's locked, and none of us have the code," Layla replied frantically.

"Oh. Well, Amy or Derek must have it; they rented this place!." Raegan said, dropping the bag and heading back into the dining room where the rest of the group was still kind of waiting around, unsure what to do.

"Amy, Derek, what's the code for the gate?" Claire said as she burst into the dining room.

"The gate isn't locked. Courtney said it would be left unlocked for the night," Amy said, feeling a mixture of scared and annoyed.

"Well, it is locked, Marco tried it, and it wouldn't budge," Layla said as tears began to well up in her eyes.

"It shouldn't be. But I have the code on my phone." Amy immediately grabbed for her phone before remembering they had locked the phones away.

"Right, the phones are all in the box. Where's the box?" Amy said, starting to panic.

"In the family room, we left the locked box in the family room," Derek said, leaving the dining room and making his way across the hall. Everyone that was left in the dining room followed him out while the rest of the party heard the commotion and made their way to the family room as well.

Derek made his way to where he had left the box. It was gone.

"Where's the box?" Lin said, looking over Derek's shoulder.

"It's gone. It was right here. Did someone move it? Who moved the box?" Derek said as he began moving things around the room. Everyone joined in and started searching the room, but there was no box anywhere to be found.

"Derek, where's the box?" Lin said again, panicking.

"I don't know. I don't know! It's not here; I left it right here. Someone must have moved it. Who moved the box?" Derek looked around the room, but everyone had the same look on their face; no one knew where the box was.

"It was a small brown box, and it was sitting right there." Asher said as he started looking under chairs.

"Wait! I have an idea!" Colleen said, running out of the room. The friends all waited in anticipation for her to return with the box but instead, "I grabbed the diffuser from the dining room; we definitely need some Zen in here." She said to a sea of rolling eyes and sighs.

"Colleen! This isn't the time for that. Get it together!" Amy said, grabbing the diffuser from Colleen's hands and slamming it down on the table.

"We should call for help; there must be a landline somewhere, right?" Bryce said, looking around the room. Nothing. "We need to check all of the rooms; they must have a phone somewhere."

The group split up and started searching the different rooms to see if they could find a phone; it didn't take long to locate a portable phone in the parlour.

"Found one!" Bryce yelled, bringing everyone to the small room at the front of the house.

Bryce picked up the phone and listened for a dial tone, nothing. "It's dead!" Bryce said, throwing the phone with frustration at a chair.

"Did you turn it on, moron?" Asher asked as he picked up the phone off of the chair.

"Easy! When's the last time you used a landline?" Bryce said, grabbing the phone back from Asher.

Bryce pressed the button to turn the phone on, but still nothing happened.

"Is it plugged in?" Claire asked, going over to the wall to check that the phone was, in fact, connected. Yup, it was dead; no landline.

"Still dead. Anyone else have another idea?" Bryce asked, throwing the phone back on the chair.

Asher suddenly had an idea, "Amy, it's only been a couple of hours since you put the code in; don't you remember it?"

"Are you serious? It was an eight-digit code that I read directly off my phone as I punched it in; why would I even think about memorizing it!" Amy was getting upset, they all were.

"Maybe there's another phone. Maybe it was just that one that was dead." Brook said, leaving the parlour and crossing the hall into the living room. There, sitting in the corner, was another phone and this one wasn't portable.

Brook ran across the room and lifted the receiver, nothing. She looked at the wall, and it was definitely connected. Looks like the phones were all down, great. "Ok, let's go back to the family room; at least there we can all sit down."

The group headed back to the family room, and everyone found a seat, everyone except for Kara, who continued pacing around the room.

"Ok, very funny. Whoever decided to put this joke together, you got us; we are all freaked out. Time to come clean." Silence, no one was owning up to the prank, if, in fact, it was a prank. Kara sat down frustrated and emotional.

"What about the notes? I don't know about the rest of you but what was written on my note isn't something that any of you could possibly know." Claire said with a touch of panic in her voice.

"Me too," Lin commented.

"Mine as well," Jack added. Everyone else nodded their heads in agreement.

"So what should we do, and what do the numbers mean? The note said something about murder and dying, are we supposed to die in that order? What is going on!" Claire was now balling her eyes out; she leaned on Mick for comfort. He lightly patted her shoulder.

"Let's not forget the fact that someone dropped off the box. Does that mean that someone else is here? That must be who locked the gate. There has to be someone else on the property." Jack said with a very shaky voice.

Everyone sat in silence for a moment listening to see if they could hear anyone else in the house. Amy suddenly started to hyperventilate; she was having a panic attack.

"Someone get her some water!" Asher called from the far side of the room. Brook was just about to leave to get the water when the lights began to flicker.

"Oh, you have got to be kidding me!" Layla said, standing up and moving towards a wall.

The lights continued to flicker for a moment as everyone started to move around in panic and then; darkness.

"Raegan, where are you?"

"Colleen, Colleen?"

"Asher, you ok?"

"Amy? Amy?"

Suddenly there was a blood-curdling scream. "Amy? Amy, where are you?" Derek called frantically.

The room was so dark, pitch black. Everyone started tripping over things and each other. It couldn't have been more than three minutes that the lights were out, but it felt like an eternity.

Suddenly the lights began to flicker again before fully coming back on. Everyone looked around the room in relief until Marco looked down and saw a trail of blood, "what the hell?!" Mick yelled while moving away from the blood. No one knew which was more shocking, the blood on the floor or Mick's reaction to it.

"Who's blood is that?" Michelle asked frantically, looking around the room to see if anyone was hurt. Everyone appeared to be ok, but someone was missing.

"Where's Amy?" Layla said, gazing around the room. "Amy! Where are you?" she yelled loudly, hoping and praying that Amy would respond.

But Amy was gone.

"Where is she? Oh god, is that her blood?" Brook said through tears. "We have to look for her; she could be hurt!" Brook continued as she sat down before she fell down.

"Or worse," Michelle added as everyone turned to look at her.

Derek couldn't take it anymore. "I have to find her. You all stay here." Derek started heading towards the door and the trail of blood.

"I'm coming with you; she's my sister," Asher said, kissing Michelle on the forehead before joining Derek at the trail of blood.

Derek and Asher looked at each other, then down at the trail of blood; time to see what was waiting at the end of the trail, good or bad.

Chapter 5
THE MURDERS

Derek and Asher started slowly down the hall, following the blood trail. The trail went past the library and the parlour; then past the front door and into the living room. Derek and Asher looked at each other; did they really want to see what was at the end of the trail?

Derek and Asher walked into the room, and there, in the middle of the floor, was Amy lying in a pool of blood. There was so much blood, way too much blood for anyone to survive. As they slowly approached the body, they heard a blood-curdling scream.

"Amy. No!!!" Layla appeared out of nowhere and pushed past Derek and Asher to get to Amy first.

Layla bent down next to Amy's body and cradled her in her arms. "Who did this to her? Who? Amy! Amy!"

Derek and Asher turned their backs on Layla and Amy; they couldn't stand seeing her like that, and Layla's reaction certainly wasn't helping. Finally, after a minute or two, Derek went over and gently removed Layla from Amy's side. Layla hugged Derek and continued to sob.

"What do we do? We can't leave her here like this." Derek said to Asher over the sound of Layla's sobs.

"But we can't move her. Someone did this to her; if we move her, we could destroy evidence. We need to catch the bastard who did this." Asher said, wiping a tear from his cheek.

"Did I? Did I destroy evidence? I didn't mean to destroy evidence. What have I done?" Layla began crying harder and harder as Derek did his best to console her.

"No, you didn't. You did what any friend would do, but now we need to get out of here before we make things worse." Derek started gently guiding Layla away from Amy's lifeless body.

Layla ran back and grabbed Amy's body, and started crying again. Asher and Derek turned their backs again to give her a moment; she clearly needed it. Both of them were deeply upset about Amy's death, but the thought of a killer in the house was certainly grabbing their attention.

After a minute or so, Derek turned around to see Layla still with Amy's body. "Come on; we need to go. The best way to help Amy now is to get to the bottom of who killed her." Derek said, helping Layla up again.

Asher was the last out of the room. He closed the door and turned off the lights, leaving his only sister's body alone in the dark. Derek, Layla and Asher walked back to the family room in the opposite direction of the blood trail they had followed. They walked past the dining room and kitchen before crossing the hallway and ending up in the family room.

As the three of them entered the family room, it was obvious that everyone had already put together what happened. "We heard Layla's scream. Is she… ok?" Brook asked, already starting to cry.

Layla immediately broke down in tears again, followed by Brook, Claire and then everyone else in the room. Not everyone cried, but there were definitely a lot of emotions going on. The group was an equal mix of sad and scared, and everything came pouring out all at once. Layla was the first to regain her composure, probably since she had had more time to process what was happening.

"We have to get out of here. Remember what the note said, ignore the murders and leave this place?!" Layla said frantically, heading back into panic mode.

"Hold on, murders? With an s? Are you sure that's what it said" Michelle walked over to Layla to ensure she had her attention.

"I, I think so. I'm pretty sure it was murders." Layla said, wiping her eyes.

"And it said something about a countdown. Is that referring to our numbers? Are we going to be murdered in that order?" Jack asked, walking over to Layla and Michelle.

"We need to have another look at that note." Lin was already out the door and on the way to the dining room. Everyone quickly followed behind her, not wanting to be the last one left in the family room. Lin looked around the table for the note with the poem, but it was gone. She searched the floor and found it lying under Raegan's chair. "Here it is." She said, standing back up.

Lin read the poem aloud again, "You've got a secret, each of you. You'll pretend it's a lie, but you know it's true. Want to keep your secrets safe? Ignore the murders and leave this place. If you decide to stay instead, the countdown is on. You're already dead." Lin finished reading the poem and looked up to see everyone staring at her.

"You were right. It was murders with an s." Michelle said shakily, "and the countdown must be referring to the order in which we will die if we don't leave. Didn't Amy say she was number one?" Michelle grabbed Amy's note that was still sitting on the table.

Yup, number one. Michelle flipped the note over to see what the secret was and nearly dropped the note in fear. "Oh my god, guys, look at this. Her note said that someone wanted her dead, and less than an hour later, she was murdered."

"And now we are all trapped in this house, and someone has numbered us all to die!" Raegan said, holding back tears.

"Who has number two?" Raegan continued reexamining the number on her own note.

"Me. I do. Looks like I'm next." Colleen said, sitting down on the chair closest to her. Everyone looked at Colleen with a mix of sadness and relief. On the one hand, no one wanted anyone else to die, but on the other hand, they were glad it wasn't them.

As soon as Colleen sat down, she started hyperventilating and shaking. Michelle was the closest to Colleen and grabbed the only glass of water left on the table. "Here, have a sip of water and take some deep breaths," Michelle said, putting a hand on Colleen's shoulder.

Colleen took a sip of water and a few deep breaths, "thanks, that helped." She said to Michelle with a forced smile.

Derek started pacing back and forth like a caged animal; finally, he couldn't take it anymore. "As much as none of us want to talk about it, I think we need to reveal what's on our notes. It may help us to determine who the murderer is. Maybe there's something in common, something we can piece together." Derek looked around the room to see that his suggestion was met with a bunch of blank stares. "Do I need to rip them out of your hands and read them myself? My wife was just murdered, and these notes have something to do with it!" Silence. No one was volunteering to read their note.

"What does yours say? You're so eager for us to tell you what our notes say; what about yours?" Mick said, getting right into Derek's face. Who was this guy? Mick's entire presence that evening was odd and kept getting odder.

"You want to know what mine says? Fine." Derek slammed his note down on the table. "I had a vasectomy."

Brook, Layla and Kara all looked at Derek with complete and utter disgust. "You had a vasectomy? Are you kidding me?" Kara said, giving Derek a shove.

"How? How could you?" Brook added, getting right in Derek's face.

Layla pushed past Brook and Kara to get right in front of Derek, "Amy has been wanting a baby for years, years! It broke her heart to keep seeing those negative pregnancy tests. How could you?" Layla backed away and tried to compose herself, Kara didn't.

"You're an asshole!" Kara slapped Derek across the face; it was satisfying.

As everyone began ganging up on Derek, something else was happening. Colleen, who had been sitting alone quietly sipping her water, suddenly shot up from her seat, grabbing her throat.

"Colleen? Colleen, what's wrong?" Marco pushed past Bryce and Jack and made his way to Colleen's side.

"Colleen, oh god! What's happening? Colleen, speak to me?" Marco said as he frantically grabbed Colleen by her shoulders.

And that's when it happened. Colleen started coughing and gasping for air frantically, then everything stopped, and her body went cold and limp.

"Colleen! Colleen! Wake up! Please wake up!" Marco said frantically, shaking Colleen. He grabbed her lifeless body and hugged her tight; she couldn't be gone; how was this possible?

After a few minutes, Marco pulled himself together. He wiped the tears from his eyes and turned to look at his supposed friends.

"Did any of you see anything? What happened? How could this possibly happen? We were all standing right here! Colleen was murdered right before our eyes." Marco picked up the glass Colleen had been drinking from a whipped it across the room.

"Which one of you did it? Who handed her that drink?" Marco started throwing plates and utensils around the room.

"I, I didn't know, I didn't know!" Michelle said shakily as she backed away from Marco. "Colleen was upset, so I handed her the only glass on the table that still had water in it, and it must have been…it must have been poisoned." Michelle was shaking so hard she could barely get the words out. Asher crossed the room and wrapped Michelle in a bear hug, trying his best to calm her down.

"Poisoned. Oh my god. What is happening? Who poisoned the water? How did they poison the water? This can't possibly be real. I don't understand." Asher hugged Michelle close, as much for himself as for her.

"Who's glass of water was it? Who brought that cup in here?" Jack asked, looking around the table to see who was missing glasses. Unfortunately, Marco's rampage made it difficult to really tell where the glass had come from.

"Who brought the water in here? Who! Which one of you did this?" Marco shouted, throwing more dishes around the room. Claire sheepishly stepped forward.

"It was me. I went to the kitchen and grabbed a glass of water from where all of the water cups were set out and put it down on the table. I had no idea it was poisoned; how could I? I mean, I was planning on drinking it." Claire started crying at the thought that it could have easily been her lying dead on the dining room floor.

The group started erupting into conversations and accusations again. Jack, who had been examining the table, managed to raise his voice enough to cut through the noise,

"Guys! Guys! Who is number 16?" Everyone paused for a moment, then turned their attention to Mick.

"Me. But you already knew that." Mick replied, sitting down calmly in a chair. Jack thought on that for a second.

"Funny, the guy that no one knows has the very last number. Who are you Mick? I think we'd like to know a little more about you." Jack paused for a moment, then turned his attention to Claire, "And funny that the person who brought Mick to the party just happened to accidentally have a drink laced with poison." Mick stood up and got between Claire and Jack. Claire gently put a hand on Mick's shoulder to move him aside.

"I brought it in for me, not for her. Michelle was the one who handed it to her. How could I have possibly known that was going to happen?" Claire started to tear up, and Mick pushed his way back in to give Jack a piece of his mind.

"Whoa, easy there, Jack. I'm just as confused by what's going on as you are. And like you said, I'm new here and don't know anyone, so why would I have a reason to kill any of you? Think you better sit down." Mick was angry.

Jack took a step back as Mick got into his face. "Ok, I think you guys both need to take a deep breath; this isn't helping anything," Derek said, getting between Mick and Jack. Jack took Derek's advice and made his way over to where Marco was sitting down next to Colleen's lifeless body. Jack was about to say something to Marco when he noticed he was holding Colleen's note in his hand.

"I. I had no idea." Marco said, dropping the note on the ground. Jack glanced down to see what Colleen's secret was, 'I had an abortion' was written on the inside of Colleen's note, and Marco was not taking the revelation well.

"Listen, why don't we go sit somewhere else and regroup? It might be easier to focus on a plan if we aren't in this room." Asher said, standing in the doorway. Everyone felt a little strange leaving the room, but they knew he was right. The group filed out one by one, leaving Marco alone with Colleen's body.

"I'm so sorry. I'm so sorry for everything." Marco kissed Colleen on the forehead and closed her eyes, then turned the lights off before leaving Colleen's body alone in the darkness.

Chapter 6
THE PANIC

The group re-entered the family room. Everyone was stressed and felt sick to their stomachs; what was happening? How did a simple birthday party turn into a mass murder event? Everyone slowly took a seat, their bodies and minds were utterly exhausted, but this wasn't the time to relax.

Everyone sat silently, staring at each other; there really was nothing to say. Finally, Derek decided enough was enough.

"I know this is awkward, but I really think we should all disclose what our notes say," Derek looked around the room, but everyone was avoiding eye contact with him. Silence.

After a long moment with no replies, Asher decided to pipe in. "Reading notes and talking about things isn't going to help us. We need to actually do something. I say we split up. Half of us look for the phones, and the other half of us try to open the gate."

The way that Asher said it, it was more of a command than a question. He looked around the group to see if everyone agreed, and everyone did, everyone but Anders.

"You guys can split up and look for the phones or try to open the gate or whatever other hopeless plan you have in mind, but according to the numbers, I'm next, so I'm staying right here. Alone." Anders grabbed one of the chairs and pushed it all the way to the far back wall and sat down facing the centre of the room; he wanted to make sure no one could sneak up on him.

"Ok, fair enough. The rest of us will split up and try and find us a way out of here." Derek said as Asher nodded in approval.

"Mick, Claire, Lin, Marco, Kara, you guys come with me to look for the phones. Michelle, Bryce, Brook, Jack, Layla and Raegan, you go with Asher to see if you can figure out a way to open the gate." Derek looked around to see what everyone thought, and no one seemed to be showing any emotion one way or the other, so he assumed they were in. Everyone took a quick moment to wish each other good luck.

Asher's group was first out of the room. Asher had no idea how they were going to get the gate open, but he was determined to try. Once Asher's group was gone, Derek turned to the remaining guests, his group.

"Ok, we need to search every inch of this house for the phones. Should we do it as a big group? Or should we split up and cover more area faster?" Derek asked, genuinely unsure of what the best answer was.

"Split up," Kara said almost immediately. "We need to get out of here; if we split up, we can cover the house much faster." Kara was very insistent on splitting up, and she was right. If they had any hope of finding the phones and getting out alive, they needed to find that box, fast.

"Ok, Mick and Claire, you take upstairs. Marco and I will take the basement, and Lin and Kara, you cover the main floor, ok?" Derek said, assigning roles to everyone, not even waiting for them to agree.

"Come on, Marco, let's go," Derek said, leaving the room with Marco hot on his heels. Both of them had already lost someone they loved and had a shared determination to get to the bottom of what was happening.

Claire and Mick left the family room and headed up the stairs to search while Lin and Kara were left on the main floor. "We have to search every inch of this floor; I'm sure the box is here somewhere," Lin said to Kara as they stood outside of the family room.

"Ok, I'm going to start in the kitchen; why don't you start in the parlour." Lin said to Kara; she nodded in agreement. The two of them split up to search their rooms alone.

Meanwhile, Marco and Derek were scouring the basement. "This basement is intense; it's way nicer than our condo and like twice as big," Marco said as he searched around the bar area.

"I know, this house is so over the top, and I still have no idea what Amy paid for it." As soon as Derek said her name, he felt a huge lump in his throat. He swallowed hard and pushed the lump down; now wasn't the time for emotions.

"What's this?" Marco said, grabbing a box from over near the billiard table. "Is that the box with the phones in it? Did you find it?" Derek ran over to see what Marco had found, hopeful it was the box they were looking for.

"I don't know, is it? It's locked, but it doesn't really look familiar, not that I looked at it that closely when I threw my phone inside." Marco said, handing the box to Derek. Derek examined the box.

"I don't know; I don't think that's it. But there's only one way to know for sure." Derek held the box above his head and threw it hard on the floor smashing the lock off the box.

"Easy!" Marco exclaimed while covering his eyes.

Derek bent down, picked the box up off the ground, and opened it. "Holy crap, it's full of drugs.

What is this place?" Marco said, grabbing a handful of baggies out of the box.

"I don't know, but there is something really off about this house. Let's keep looking." Derek took the baggies out of Marco's hand, put them back in the box, then closed it and returned it to where Marco found it. The two gave each other a 'don't you dare' look, then went back to searching the basement.

Derek went towards the large sitting room while Marco made his way back to the bar area. The two of them hadn't resumed their search for more than a minute before they heard a horrible scream coming from the floor above them. They immediately dropped what they were doing and ran upstairs to see what had happened.

While Derek and Marco searched the basement, Claire and Mick were busy upstairs searching the bedrooms for the box. Claire took the bedrooms on the left while Mick searched the bedrooms on the right. There were nine bedrooms in the house, so it was no small feat to inspect them all thoroughly.

Claire, being Claire, worked very precisely opening every drawer carefully and gently moving items, looking under the bed and inside the closet, then going through the luggage in the room without disturbing anything. She was halfway through the first room when Mick burst in to see how it was going.

"Any luck?" He said, sticking his head into the room.

"Not yet, but I'm halfway through this room," Claire said as she meticulously put someone's clothes back in their bag.

"Well, there's nothing in any of those ones," Mick said, pointing across the hall.

"What? How could you know that already? We've only been searching for like 10 minutes." Claire said, leaving the room she was in and walking across the hall.

She entered the room directly across from where she was and immediately knew how Mick was done so fast; the room was absolutely trashed. Every drawer was dumped on the floor, the covers were thrown off the bed, and the overnight bag was emptied all over the ground. Claire looked at Mick, who winked at her, "I don't mess around." He said as he headed back to Claire's side of the hall to search the next room.

Mick's style was certainly different from Claire's, but she couldn't argue with his effectiveness. Claire went back to finish searching the first bedroom when she heard a blood-curdling scream from the floor below. She ran out of the room and joined Mick in the hall. The two of them quickly ran downstairs to see what was going on.

On the main floor, everything started just fine but went downhill quickly. As discussed, Lin went to the kitchen to search for the box while Kara was to make her way to the parlour. Unfortunately, that wasn't exactly what happened.

Once Lin was out of sight, Kara snuck into the family room to have a moment alone with Anders, Lin's husband.

"Hey," Kara said, entering the family room causing Anders to jump.

"Oh, hey, you startled me." He said, relaxing once he realized who it was.

Kara walked across the room and showed Anders her note; it read, 'you are in love with Anders.' Anders pulled out his note, 'you are in love with Kara.' The two of them locked eyes as Kara let out a muffled sob.

"Anders, I'm so scared. I don't want you to die. You can't die." Kara said as Anders leaned in to give her a hug.

"How could this maniac have known about us? I don't understand." Kara continued as she cried into Anders's shoulder.

Kara and Anders embraced for another few moments until Kara was able to regain her composure.

"I just wanted to say be careful. I love you." Kara said, squeezing Anders tightly.

" I love you too." Anders said as he leaned in to kiss Kara.

"What the hell is going on?" Lin yelled from the doorway where she'd been watching the whole thing. Kara and Anders separated as quickly as humanly possible, but it was too late; Lin had seen everything. Anders moved Kara aside and got between her and Lin; there was no point lying anymore, so he figured he might as well come out with the whole truth and get it over with.

"Lin. Kara and I are in love. We've been having an affair for six months." Anders said, putting his note on the side table between himself and Line. He then took a step back and braced himself for what was inevitably going to come next.

Lin looked at the note on the table, then back up and Anders. She then reached into her pocket, pulled out her note and slapped it on the table next to Anders'. Anders leaned in to read it,

"You're pregnant? You're pregnant? Seriously? Who's the father?" As the words left Anders' mouth and he immediately regretted them.

"Who's the father? You are you, asshole!" Lin grabbed a lamp off a nearby table and whipped it at the wall, breaking it.

"And you!" Lin lunged at Kara, nearly knocking her off her feet. "Get out of here! Leave!"

Anders grabbed Lin to hold her back while nodding to Kara to leave the room. Kara didn't feel great about leaving Anders alone with Lin in that state, but she reluctantly left. Lin broke free from Anders' grasp and walked across the room.

"How could you? Honestly? How could you do this to me?" Lin said while kicking and shoving things all over the room, completely trashing it.

"I'm sorry, Lin, but this can't come as the much of a shock to you. We haven't been happy in a long time. I'm sorry you found out this way, but it's time you found out." Anders walked over and put a hand on Lin's shoulder, and that was the last straw.

Lin snapped. She turned around to face Anders, grabbed a statue sitting on the table closest to her and hit Anders on the head hard enough to not only knock him out but to kill him.

Kara, who had been listening outside in the hall, heard the commotion and rushed back in to see what had happened. She took one look at Anders lying on the floor, and she screamed at the top of her lungs, "Anders! Oh god! No!"

Kara rushed over and cradled Anders' lifeless body in her arms while Kara stood over the both of them, still holding the statue.

Of course, Kara's scream was enough to get the attention of the others who had been searching for the phone and thankfully, they arrived moments later, not a moment too soon. Claire and Mick were the first ones in the room, followed closely by Marco and Derek.

As soon as Lin realized that the others had entered the room, she dropped the statue and immediately poured on the grieving widow act. "Thank god you're here! She was just about to kill me, just like she did Anders. I was ready to defend myself if I had to, but thankfully it didn't come to that." Lin began to sob and threw herself into Derek's arms.

"What are you talking about, you crazy bitch?! You killed him. You killed Anders. All because he wanted to leave you." Kara said while holding Anders' lifeless body.

Claire picked up the notes off the table and showed them to Marco and Derek. Derek immediately went from comforting Lin to restraining her.

"Derek? What are you doing? This is all Kara's fault. All of it. She ruined my life. She ruined it!" Lin frantically tried to get out of Derek's grip, but he was holding her tight.

"Let go of me!" Lin squirmed the best she could, but Derek wasn't about to let go of her, not after they'd caught her red-handed.

Marco stepped forward and got into Lin's face. "You murdered him because he cheated on you, but why did you kill Amy and Colleen? They were your friends. What did they ever do to you?" Marco had to hold himself back from slapping Lin in the face; it wasn't easy.

"What? I had nothing to do with their deaths. I'm not a murderer." Everyone glared at Lin. "I mean, other than this one time. And he had it coming." Lin conceded the fact that she was a murderer but wasn't willing to admit that she was a mass murderer.

"Where are the phones, Lin? Just let us go, please?" Claire said, trying to appeal to Lin's good nature if there was any good nature left.

"I have no idea. I had nothing to with the other deaths; I'm as in the dark as the rest of you. The only reason I caught these two love birds was because I was looking to find Kara to tell her what I discovered in the kitchen." Lin stopped talking as the others waited expectantly.

"What?" Derek said frustratedly.

"The back door to the house is unlocked, so anyone could have come in or out at any point. I'm not the bad guy in all of this; I was just trying to help!" Lin was really pouring it on now, even though she clearly was the bad guy or at least one of the bad guys.

Derek took a deep breath. "I think the best idea is to lock Lin up in one of the bedrooms until we know more about what's going on."

Everyone nodded in agreement, even Lin. "Sure, might as well lock me in a room by myself; if things keep going the way they are, I don't have much time left anyway."

Derek let go of Lin's arms. She straightened her clothes, fixed her hair, then walked out of the room toward the staircase; Marco, Mick and Derek followed her out while Claire stayed with Kara, trying to give her at least a little comfort.

As Lin walked up the stairs, she immediately saw the total destruction of all of the bedrooms on the right where Mick had been 'searching.'

"I'm not going in any of those rooms; I'll take this one, thank you very much." Lin walked into the first bedroom on the left, the one that was supposed to be for Layla and Raegan slammed the door behind her and locked it from the inside.

"Don't worry; I'm not coming out, promise." She said from the other side of the door.

Derek stepped away from the room that now had Lin inside and called Marco and Mick into a huddle. "I don't think she's going anywhere, but maybe one of us should stay outside the door just to be safe. Mick, can you do it?" Mick nodded yes, grabbed a chair from the room next door and took a seat outside Lin's room/jail cell.

"Should we go back to looking for the phones?" Marco said to Derek as the two of them started downstairs. No sooner had they reached the main floor when screams filled the air, this time from outside. They looked to the family room to see that Claire and Kara were in the hall, both looking as terrified as the screams sounded.

The four of them rushed to the front door to
see what in the hell was happening outside.

Chapter 7
THE GATE

While the group searched the house for the box with the phones, the others went outside to see if they could figure out how to open the gate. Michelle, Asher, Raegan, Layla, Jack, Brook and Bryce headed out the front door and walked over to the still very will locked gate. As soon as Jack got to the gate, he started shaking it back and forth, maybe there was a mistake, and it wasn't really locked. No matter how hard Jack shook the gate, it didn't move, not even an inch.

"That gate is intense; I don't think there's any way we are going to be able to break it open," Brook said as Jack continued trying to shake it loose.

"We need another plan," Asher said, backing away from the gate. "This piece of property must be huge; the fence goes as far as I can see in either direction and, as far as I can tell, surrounds the entire property. Brook, Bryce, why don't you attempt to walk the perimeter to see if there are any openings anywhere." Brook and Bryce nodded; they were on it.

As Brook and Bryce headed off to explore the perimeter, Asher went back to giving out jobs.

"Layla, Raegan, Michelle, can you see if there's any way to tamper with the pin pad? Maybe we can bypass it or break it somehow, forcing the gate to open." Michelle, Layla and Raegan looked at each; they were ready to give it a try.

"So that leaves you and me, Jack. I think we need to see if we can somehow climb over the fence." Asher looked up to the top of the fence; it was at least 15 feet tall and totally smooth. The fence around the property was just as tall as well; this place was a fortress.

"And how are we supposed to do that? And even if we manage to get over the fence, what exactly are we supposed to do? It's late, and this house is in the middle of nowhere." Jack said, surveying the height of the gate.

"Got a better idea?" Asher said while heading towards his car.

"Where are you going?" Jack called to him as he walked away. Asher got into his car and drove it towards the gate; Jack moved to the side to let him pull up right next to the gate.

"We're gonna stand on top of the car to give us some extra height," Asher said, jumping onto the hood of his car. Jack wasn't sure about this idea, but he joined Asher on the hood and then on the roof.

While Jack and Asher attempted to get over the gate, Brook and Bryce attempted to find a way through it.

"This fence is ridiculous. Who needs a fence this big and this high around their entire property?" Brook said as the two of them finally reached the first corner. They turned around to see the house way in the far distance.

"Shall we keep going?" Brook said to Bryce, who shrugged and nodded yes.

"You're unusually quiet tonight. I would ask what's wrong, but I think the answer is pretty obvious." More silence from Bryce, so Brook continued.

"It's funny how people deal with these situations so differently. I mean, here you are, not saying a word, walking around in total silence and me? I can't stop talking. It's almost like I feel like if I stop talking, I might die. Like, somehow, if I keep talking and talking, the killer can't get me. I know it doesn't make sense like I get that, but having two friends murdered in the space of 30 minutes is really messing with my brain. Do you know what I mean? I mean, you get me, right Bryce." Bryce gave Brook a half smile as they continued to walk.

"I really appreciate it. Knowing that you're here with me makes me feel so much better, so much safer. Ya know? I hope being with me does that same thing for you, like being your safe person is so important to me, it really is." Brook was so busy rambling that she didn't realize Bryce had stopped walking.

"Brook," Bryce said in a loud whisper. "Brook!" He said louder, finally getting her attention.

"What? Did you find something?" Brook went to where Bryce was standing.

"Do you see that light over there?" Bryce said, pointing to a small light in the distance.

"Yes! Is it moving? It looks like it's moving." Brook said in a not-so-whispery whisper.

"I think it's a flashlight; someone's out there," Bryce whispered to Brook. As the two of them looked to see if they could determine what was going on, the light suddenly swept in their direction. Bryce pulled Brook down to the ground and out of sight.

"Do you think it's the murderer?" Brook whispered to Bryce, her voice shaking.

"How am I supposed to know?" Bryce said to Brook while also pulling her back down to the ground.

"We need to tell the others." Brook went to stand back up, but Bryce stopped her. The flashlight was now pointed in their direction and moving closer. Suddenly the light stopped, turned and went in the complete opposite direction. Brook and Bryce remained silently on the ground for another few moments before carefully and quietly getting up.

"We need to finish searching the perimeter and quickly. If there's a break anywhere, then someone has probably been coming and going from the house all night." Bryce said as he started into a jog.

"Right! Gotta keep those eyes open. Looking for gaps. Looking for gaps." Brook attempted to jog behind Bryce for about 30 seconds before returning to a walk.

"You go on ahead; I'm right behind you!" Brook said, already sounding out of breath.

"Come on, Brooky. You can do it! I'm not leaving you behind, and we need to move fast; this could be the difference between life and death." Bryce grabbed Brook's hand and pulled her along. She dramatically jogged behind Bryce as they scanned the fence for any sign of an opening.

While Brook and Bryce inspected the fence, Michelle, Layla, and Raegan were trying, unsuccessfully, to get the gate to open via the pin pad.

"This is nuts; I know nothing about this kind of stuff, nothing!" Layla said in total frustration. "This is my area of expertise, and I don't even know where to begin. This is one of the most complicated systems

I've ever seen." Raegan said while trying one of the many universal reset codes.

"Your area of expertise? What exactly do you do?" Michelle asked as she watched from a bit of a distance.

"I'm the Manager of Tech Support for a security firm. I manage a team that deals with people having technical issues with their security systems. But this one is different from anything I've ever seen." Raegan was totally stumped by this system; it wasn't like anything else on the market.

"I wonder where they got it from; it must have been a totally custom job," Raegan said, trying yet another useless code.

"Can we, like, smash it open? Like if we break it, will that work?" Michelle asked while searching for some kind of rock to use.

"No. Unfortunately, that won't work. Without the code, we are totally locked out. Or, in this case, in." Raegan pushed another button, and something happened.

"Hold on, what's this?" A screen had come up that showed a log of when the password had been most recently entered.

"Look, someone used the password after all of us arrived. Someone else is here, or they were here." Raegan looked at Michelle and Layla, both of whom were staring at her, confused and terrified.

Brook and Bryce were finally at the back wall of the fence, and that's where they found it.

"Bryce, look!" Brook had found an opening in the fence, which wasn't large, but maybe a determined person could squeeze through.

"One of the fence polls is missing; someone could have gotten in and out without us knowing," Brook said, examining the size of the gap.

"It's small, but it's possible." Brook continued attempting to squeeze through, but she couldn't do it.

"It would need to be someone really skinny; neither of us could fit through that gap," Bryce said, examining the gap closer.

"Kara! Kara could fit through that gap. We should get her to go through the fence and see if she can get help!" Brook was excited, finally a light at the end of the tunnel.

"Ok, let's keep searching. If we found one spot, there might be another." Bryce wasn't sure the small gap in the fence was the revelation Brook thought it was.

"What room is that?" Brook asked, pointing to the house. It was far away, but there was a backdoor with a light over it.

"The kitchen?" Bryce wasn't sure, but he was pretty positive there was a backdoor in the kitchen.

"Oh, that's perfect, perfect! Kara will be able to go from the kitchen to the fence and get us out of here!" Brook was way more excited than Bryce was, but any sliver of hope was a good thing at this point.

"Let's just finish our check." Bryce started jogging along the fence again, and Brook was right beside him; the new shot of adrenaline from finding the hole gave her the energy she needed to finish inspecting the fence.

"Ok, can you boost my foot at all?" Asher asked Jack as the two of them stood on top of his car.

"I mean, I can try, but even if you do get to the top, how are you going to get down on the other side?" Jack was right; even if, by some miracle, they got Asher to the top of the gate, there was no way he could land safely on the other side. From the distance he would have to drop down, he would at least sprain an ankle, if not worse.

"Damn!" I thought we were so close. Asher and Jack sat on the roof of the car, feeling defeated. Michelle walked over from where she had been working with Layla and Raegan to try and open the gate using the pin pad.

"No luck?" Michelle asked, already knowing the answer.

"No. Even if we could get over the gate, there's no way we could drop down safely on the other side." Asher said, kicking the roof of his car.

"Mich, can you pass me my water bottle? It should be in the car." Michelle opened the car door, reached inside and grabbed Asher's water bottle from the cup holder.

"Here." She said, passing it to him. Asher took a big sip then Jack and Asher got down from the roof.

"Asher! Michelle! Guys!" Asher and Michelle turned around to see Brook and Bryce jogging towards them in the distance as Brook called their names.

"You're never going to believe what we found." Brook and Bryce finished jogging and met up with the rest of the group. Raegan and Layla were the first to get to them, with Jack, Michelle and finally, Asher trailing behind.

"What? Did you find something?" Layla asked excitedly.

"So much! So much stuff happened!" Brook said before looking to Bryce to fill in the details. Bryce told everyone about the light in the distance and the opening in the fence, and he was just about to tell them about the access through the kitchen when Asher dropped to the ground and started convulsing.

"Asher? Asher, oh my god!" Michelle pushed past everyone and was the first to get to Asher, who was now lying on the ground, lifeless and foaming from the mouth.

"He's dead! He's dead!" She screamed as she rocked back and forth, holding Asher's body.

The commotion outside brought the inside group out to see what was going on. Marco and Derek were the first outside, with Claire and Kara right behind them. Mick, of course, was busy watching over Lin while she was locked in her room upstairs.

"What? What's going on?" Derek yelled as he parted the group and saw Asher lying cold and lifeless on the ground.

"What happened?" He asked, kneeling down beside Michelle.

"Look at his mouth; I think he was poisoned," Marco said, pointing to the white foam dripping from the side of Asher's mouth.

The group started moving closer to take a better look, and that's when the sky opened. Rain started coming down in buckets, the wind picked up, and thunder and lightning filled the sky.

"We gotta go back inside; come on," Layla said, getting up and dragging Raegan behind her; everyone else followed them inside except for Derek and Michelle.

"Michelle, we gotta go," Derek said, grabbing Michelle's hand and helping her up.

"I can't. I can't leave him here!" Michelle screamed, still holding onto Asher's hand.

"Asher's dead, Michelle. You can't help him now." Derek pried Michelle's hands-free, and the two of them ran inside out of the rain.

THE EMOTIONS

The exhausted and now soaking-wet friends dragged themselves back into the house and exhaustedly slumped down in the front hall. "Why? Why did the killer tell us to leave? We can't leave! We are never going to get out of here! We are all gonna die!" Raegan was hysterical. Layla did her best to comfort her, but Raegan was having none of it.

Derek decided enough was enough and stood up to try to persuade everyone one more time to share their notes, "Ok, we're tried searching, we've tried escaping, and it isn't working. Four people are already dead, and the murderer doesn't seem to be stopping…." Derek was about to continue when Jack interrupted him. "Four? Who else is dead?"

Derek cleared his throat; so much had happened in the last few minutes that he forgot that half of the group had no idea Anders was also dead. "Anders. Lin murdered him in the family room after finding out he was in love with Kara." Derek said, breaking the news.

"He was in love with Kara? Kara, were you in love with him?" Jack asked, feeling more than a little heartbroken.

"Yes, Jack, I loved Anders. I love Anders." Kara said, starting to break down. Even though Kara and Jack had never been a couple, the realization that Kara loved someone else was a slap in the face.

"Hold up; Lin murdered Anders? Where is she? You mean we caught the murderer?" Bryce said with a mix of anger and excitement.

"I'm not so sure. I don't think she killed Amy, and Colleen and Asher died after we had already locked her in the room. I think it might have been more of an instant impulse situation." Marco said, starting to feel that perhaps Lin wasn't the murderer they thought she was.

"But Anders was number three, wasn't he? Pretty big coincidence that he died in the right order." Layla chimed in, making a very good point.

"Who's next?" Claire asked, looking around at the group.

"Me, I'm number five," Kara said with a shaky voice.

Derek cleared his throat in an attempt to regain everyone's attention. It took a moment, but everyone eventually moved their attention back to Derek.

"I know no one wants to, but I think it's finally time for us to reveal what's on our notes. I said it before, and I'll say it again, the only way to figure out who the murderer is is to figure out who could possibly know these things about us. Besides, we will all end up finding out what was on the notes one way or another. Wouldn't it be better to be alive when that happens?" Derek really hoped his speech would work this time, but he wasn't sure if he had gotten through.

"Fine, you're right. We all know you're right. Can we at least go and change first? We're soaked to the bone, and I want nothing more than to get out of these ridiculous clothes." Layla said, standing up and ringing out her top.

"Yes, good idea. Let's all go upstairs and change; then, we can sit in the basement and try and figure this out. I don't know about you guys, but I'd rather be on the floor with no dead bodies." Derek got up and headed towards the stairs; everyone followed him. It was like a depressing parade full of sad, soaking-wet, exhausted partygoers from the wrong decade.

As Derek arrived at the top of the stairs, he made eye contact with Mick. "What's going on?" Mick asked, seeing everyone file one by one up the stairs.

"Asher's dead. Poisoned. He died outside by the gate right before the storm started. We're all getting changed; then we're going to reveal what's on our notes to see if we can figure out the connection." Derek said with a big sigh.

"Man, what the hell is going on? Lin hasn't left the room, so I don't think she's responsible unless she poisoned him earlier. I mean, it's possible." Mick said, leaning back on his chair.

"Um, Mick, that's our room; we need to get in there," Layla said with an arm around Raegan, still trying to calm her down.

"No can do, but I think one of the rooms on the other side is free; here's your stuff." Mick picked a bag up off the floor and threw it to Layla, who didn't catch it. She picked the bag up off the floor.

Michelle opened the door to her bedroom. "What? What the hell happened in here?" The room was a complete disaster from Mick's earlier search.

"That's on me. I was searching for the box with the phones; everything's still in there, though; just step over the crap." Mick yelled from down the hall. Michelle rolled her eyes, stepped over the pile and closed the door behind her.

Layla and Raegan took their stuff into the empty and very messy bedroom while everyone else entered their room and shut the door. Jack and Kara were the last ones to go into their room.

Kara started going through the piles until she found herself a change of clothes. She picked her shirt and sweatpants up off the floor and headed toward the bathroom to change.

"How you holding up?" Jack asked, standing between Kara and the door.

"I've been better." She said, trying to move around him.

Kara moved to walk around Jack, who sidestepped to get back between Kara and the bathroom door.

"You know, if you need anything, I'm here. I'm always here for you." Jack put his arms out, and Kara reluctantly stepped into a hug. Kara tolerated the hug for a few moments before attempting to back up. Unfortunately, Jack was less than great at reading signals and rather than letting her go, he went in for a kiss.

"Are you kidding me?" Kara forcefully pushed Jack away and stepped past him. "You literally just heard me tell the story of watching Anders, the man I love, murdered before my eyes, and you thought this was a good opportunity to go in for a kiss?!" Kara stormed into the bathroom, shut the door and locked it.

Jack slumped down on the bed. He couldn't believe he'd misread the situation so badly. He quickly grabbed his clothes off the floor, changed and left the room; he didn't want to be there when Kara came out of the bathroom.

Layla and Raegan were in their new room, next door to Kara and Jack, trying to compose themselves before going back out into the hall with the others. "Do you want to talk about it?" Raegan asked, having regained her composure from earlier.

"About what?" Layla asked, genuinely confused about which aspect of this godawful evening Raegan was referring to.

"About your best friend being brutally murdered and you finding the body." Raegan continued putting a hand on Layla's shoulder. Layla turned and faced Raegan.

"Honestly? No, I don't. I'm worried that if I start to talk about it, I'm going to break down, and that can't happen right now, not until we are out of here and safe. I will have plenty of time to grieve properly and process this night but not right now." Raegan pulled Layla in for a hug and kissed her on the forehead. A tear rolled down Layla's cheek.

Once everyone had finished changing, they met again at the top of the stairs. "Ok, everyone ready?" Derek said to the group of shaken partygoers. "Let's head to the basement." Derek was the first one down the stairs, followed by Marco, Michelle, Layla and Raegan. Jack looked back to see if Kara was coming, but she purposely avoided eye contact with him, so he started down without her. Brook and Bryce were the next ones down, leaving Claire, Kara and Mick alone upstairs.

"Do not leave that spot," Kara said to Mick.

"She is insane, and if she gets out, I know she's going to try and kill me." Mick gave Kara a reassuring nod as she and Claire headed down the stairs to join the others in the basement.

Chapter 9
THE SECRETS

Derek turned on the lights in the basement and led everyone toward the sitting room that he and Marco had explored earlier. As everyone took a seat, Brook could feel the eyes on her and her somewhat tone-deaf outfit of a hot pink crop top that said 'Bad Bitch' matched to hot pink leggings.

"Look, I know my outfit is not super appropriate, but it's all I brought. This was supposed to be a party, not a funeral!" Brook said, sitting down.

"Did everyone bring their notes with them?" Derek asked, taking his note out of his pocket. Everyone reluctantly removed their notes from their pockets and held them up.

"Well, you all already know what my secret is." Derek placed his note down on the coffee table with the 'you had a vasectomy' revelation facing up. "Who's next? Should we go in order?" Derek continued.

"You mean the order in which we're slated to be murdered?" Kara asked dramatically. "Well, I'm next. But I think you all already know my secret at this point. I'm in love with Anders, and he is, was, in love with me. I'm the reason he was murdered." Kara put her note down on the table, and her mind rushed back to the night she and Anders admitted they were in love.

"I remember the night that Anders and I really knew we were in love. It was about four months ago, and Anders and I were hanging out in my apartment the same way we did every Thursday night. Anders told Lin he was in a hockey league, so he always had an excuse to come to my place so we could be together. We were sitting on the couch watching a movie, sipping wine and eating popcorn; it was our favourite thing to do together. I remember Anders leaned in to kiss me just as his phone buzzed. It was Lin asking him some inane question. Neither he nor Lin wanted to admit anything out loud, but she knew something was up. When Anders turned off his phone, looked me in the eye, and told me he loved me, that was it. That was the moment I knew in my heart he had chosen me over Lin; that was the moment that I fell head over heels in love." Kara had barely finished her story when she started sobbing again. Jack reached over to comfort her, but she quickly moved away.

"But I never told anyone about our relationship, never. And I know he never did either. I don't know how anyone could have possibly known about it. I feel so violated." Kara said, sitting back and giving the floor to the next victim.

Michelle reached forward and put her note down on the table face up. She didn't read it aloud, but she made sure everyone could see what it said, 'you tried to commit suicide.'.

"It was six months ago. I remember standing in the bathroom looking down at the note I had written to Asher, telling him how sorry I was but couldn't live like that anymore. I had been saving up prescription pills for months, taking a little bit less than I was prescribed every day and putting the extra into a pill container. Finally, I had collected enough to constitute a fatal dose. I remember swallowing the pills in one gulp without even using water. I looked at myself in the mirror and watched as my world started to go black, then suddenly, something went off inside of me. Suddenly I wanted to live more than I wanted to die for the first time in I don't know how long. I remember I was close to losing consciousness, but I managed to stick my fingers down my throat and vomit the pills out of my system. I barfed and barfed and barfed until my insides were emptied, then I sat huddled on the floor, alive but a total mess. As I lay on the floor shaking, I heard Asher at the door. He asked me gently if I was all right, and all I could squeak out was, I'm fine. I never told him what I had done. I never told anyone."

Michelle sat down next to Kara, who put an arm around her to comfort her. Raegan stood up; she was the next to share her shame. She looked at Layla and mouthed the words, 'I love you,' before putting her note down next to the others. "I've been stealing security codes." Raegan said to the group, "I'm sorry I know it's wrong, but our lifestyle is so expensive, and I hate letting you down." She said to Layla, who was sitting there dumbfounded.

"To be honest, it wasn't that I was keeping it from you exactly; it's just not something that's easy to bring up in conversation. It all started about six months ago. We had started going out more for dinner and planning an expensive vacation, and we just didn't have the money to cover everything. But I didn't want to let you down, I wanted you to have everything you ever wanted. I still want that. One day, a man approached me and told me he would pay me a lot of money if I could provide him a few security codes. So I did it. I felt sick to my stomach about it, but then I saw that the man was arrested and that the owners were fine, and somehow it made me feel better about selling the codes. I've only done it a few times and no one has ever gotten hurt, but I promise you I will never do it again. " Raegan sat down and looked to Layla for reassurance. Layla pulled Raegan into a hug which Raegan gladly accepted.

Everyone sat quietly, waiting for the next person to go, but no one was stepping forward. Finally, Derek spoke up, "I'm next, but you all already know my secret, I had a vasectomy."

"Derek, how long ago did you get your vasectomy?" Marco asked curiously.

"It was about six months ago; why?" He replied.

"It seems like, so far, all of the stories have happened in the last six months. I was just curious if yours was as well.

"Ya. In hindsight, it might not have been the right decision, but I'm just not ready for kids, I'm not. My doctor told me it could always be reversed, so I figured I would get it done now; then, if I decided to have kids, I would get it reversed, and Amy would never know the difference. I'm not proud of my decision, but I can't change it now." Everyone glared at Derek, shocked by his selfishness but they had more pressing matters to deal with. "Who's next?"

Once again, silence. After a long awkward moment, Kara spoke up, "I think Lin is next, but since she's not here, I'll tell you her secret. She's pregnant, and it can't be more than a few months since none of us could tell." With every revelation, the tension in the room grew. How could every one of them have such intense secrets?

Claire stood up. It was her turn to go. "I was a stripper to put myself through college. And I never stopped." Everyone looked at Claire, urging her to continue; the more details they shared, the better their chances of figuring out a common thread through all of their secrets.

"I mean, technically, I did stop, I stopped for a few years after I graduated school, but about three months ago I started again. I had been living off my salary just fine, but then the landlord raised my rent, and I had to decide between losing my home or taking on a second job. Well, I decided to take a second job, and I haven't looked back since. I mean, ya, I don't love people knowing this, I haven't admitted it to anyone yet, but I'm also not really ashamed of it either. You gotta do what you gotta do to support yourself, ya know?" Claire sat down feeling energized; she was the only one who didn't seem to be utterly mortified by her secret.

Bryce was up next, "I hate to break the trend but my note is about something that happened years ago." Bryce laid his note down on the table without saying anything. Everyone leaned in to see what the note said. 'You physically abused your ex-girlfriend.'

Brook looked at Bryce, "Is that, is that true?" Brook was now standing, looking down at Bryce.

"No. I mean, yes, technically, it's true, but she came at me first. We were living together in College, and I got home late one night. We'd both been drinking, and she was mad that I hadn't bothered to text her to let her know where I was. She came at me and started punching and kicking me, and I shoved her off of me. When she fell back, she hit her head on a table and ended up bleeding everywhere. The cops came and arrested me, and I never saw her again. I moved away, cut ties with everyone who knew about what happened and never spoke of it again. It was over ten years ago." Bryce finished and Brook sat back down beside him. She wasn't sure exactly how she felt about his story but decided that now wasn't the time to fight about it.

"Ok. I'm next." Marco said, adding his note to the pile. "I spent time in jail." Kara's eyes went wide,

"You spent time in jail? When? For what?" She asked, mildly freaking out.

"I didn't realize we were asking questions," Marco replied, throwing attitude Kara's way.

"Well, I think given the circumstances of the evening, my question is valid," Kara replied, looking around the room for encouragement from everyone else.

"All right, you want to know why I was in jail? I'll tell you. I got arrested when I was 17 years old for armed robbery and spent six months in jail. And since I was a juvenile, it isn't on my record. I've never told anyone about it, not even Colleen, so I have no idea how whoever wrote these notes found out about it. Happy now?" Marco looked at Kara to see her reaction.

"No. But I'm glad you weren't in jail for, like, attempted murder or something." Kara said to Marco with a forced smile.

"My turn," Jack said walking over and putting his note down on the table. "I cheated my way into my job."

Everyone looked at Jack. In the grand scheme of revelations, his didn't seem like that big of a deal. "I was finishing up my 3rd year of University when my funds ran dry. I started applying for jobs online, but anything I was qualified for just wouldn't pay enough to cover my bills. So, I doctored my resume, and instead of finishing my 3rd year of University, I put that I had completed my master's. Well, I got an interview, then I got a job, and I just kept working. I never went back and completed my degree let alone got my master's and if anyone finds that out I'm done for." Jack went back to his seat and looked at Kara; she immediately turned away, she couldn't even make eye contact with him.

"So, who's left? Layla? I think you're next, right?" Derek said, looking at Layla, whose eyes were all red and puffy. Layla turned to Raegan and grabbed her hand. "Before I show my note, I need you to know that I love you so much. I have always loved you, and I will always love you."

Layla put her note on the table and read it aloud, "I'm in love with Amy. But let me, let me explain. This isn't anything I ever acted on or that Amy even knew about. I tried to tell her several times just because I needed to get it off my chest, but I never could. I'm so sorry, Raegan. I don't know what to say other than I'm sorry, and I never meant to hurt you." Layla sat back next to Raegan and grabbed her hand. Raegan went to pull away but didn't; now wasn't the time.

"My turn. I'm addicted to painkillers." Brook put her note down on the table and sat back down.

"It all started six months ago when I hurt my back. My doctor prescribed my painkillers, and now I can't start my day or end my day without two painkillers. It's awful. When I started, I was taking half a pill once a day, but slowly I started needing more and more. I can't stop. I don't know how to stop. And I think it's going to keep getting worse. No one, I mean no one knows about this; I've never told a living soul." Brook sat down and looked to Bryce, who hugged her hard.

Derek looked around the room. "Ok, so that's all of us, and we're missing five notes. Amy's, but we know her note said someone wants her dead. Then there was Colleen's note that said she had an abortion. Lin's said she was pregnant, and Anders' said he was in love with Kara. So that leaves Mick and Asher." Derek turned to Michelle, "Did you grab Asher's note?"

Michelle shook her head no. "No, I didn't think to. Should I have? Oh god! It's probably been destroyed by the rain!"

"Don't worry, we will see what Mick's note says and maybe we can figure something that ties everything together. Because right now, I can't see any pattern other than the fact that all of us had a secret we didn't want to be exposed and somehow, someone found that out." Derek was now standing and starting to make his way toward the stairs. "Let's go see what Mick's note said."

Chapter 10

THE MYSTERY MAN

Derek led the group out of the basement to the main floor, then upstairs to where Mick was sitting in the hall outside of the room; Lin was locked inside. Asleep.

"Mick!" Derek called out, causing Mick to twitch but not wake up.

"Mick!" He said again, shaking him awake. Mick startled awake and almost punched Derek in the face.

"Wha..what's going on?" Mick blinked hard and focused his eyes. It took him a moment to fully wake up and realize everyone was there, staring at him.

"How are you asleep? Four people are dead, murdered, and you're napping like nothing's happening." Raegan said, almost in tears.

"You seem pretty relaxed for someone who claims to be innocent. The rest of us are turning around, watching our backs, terrified we're about to be murdered, and here you are having a little ol' snooze!" Bryce said, getting right into Mick's face.

"You left me alone in a hallway. I got bored and passed out, end of story." Mick said, standing up and getting right into Bryce's face.

"Where's Lin?" Derek asked over the commotion.

"Where's Lin?" He asked again louder.

"What do you mean, where's Lin? She's in the bedroom, right where you left her." Mick stepped aside so Derek could go in and see for himself. Derek went to open the door, but it was locked.

"Lin." Derek pounded on the door. "Lin, open up." Derek knocked again, hard, but there was still no answer.

"Lin! Lin!" Derek pounded on the door. He then took a step back and started kicking it to break it down. Kick. Kick. Kick. On the third kick, the door opened, revealing Lin hanging from the ceiling fan with a chair knocked over just below her feet and her note on the ground.

Derek was the first one inside, followed by Marco and Jack. Brook was next through the door. "Oh my god! Lin! Did she do this to herself? I don't understand." Brook picked her note up off the ground. "Lin was pregnant, just like Kara said. But look at this, her number was crossed out and changed to number 5. Do you think she did this herself?"

Everyone looked at Mick. "I never moved. No one was in or out of the room." Mick said, reading everyone's minds.

"Except you," Jack said from across the room.

"What'd you say?" Mick said, walking towards Jack.

"Except for you," Jack said again, a little less forcefully.

Mick poked Jack in the chest, "I. Never. Went. In." Jack started to back up but decided against it; he was done being a pushover.

"How are we supposed to know that? You could have easily gone in, killed Lin and then come back out." Jack said with an intensity that none of the others had ever heard from him.

"What does your note say?" Derek said, stepping between Jack and Mick.

"What? Why?" Mick said, getting defensive.

"We've all shared our notes. We've all shared our secrets, your turn." Derek said, changing his tone; he was no longer asking; he was demanding.

Mick took his note out of his pocket and held it in his hand. He then crumpled it up and threw it in Derek's face. Derek picked the note up off the ground and uncrumpled it.

"You aren't who you say you are," Derek said, reading the note aloud.

"You aren't who you say you are; what does that mean?" Jack said, taking a step closer to Mick.

"How am I supposed to know? I didn't write it." Mick said defensively.

Raegan, who had been listening from the hall, suddenly piped in on the conversation. "Are you sure about that? Everyone else here tonight knows each other. Everyone but you." Raegan lunged toward Mick and Marco had to hold her back.

"Come on. That's not entirely true," Claire said, jumping to Mick's defence.

"I know Mick; I'm the one who invited him here." Raegan got out of Marco's grip and made her way over to Claire.

"But how well do you really know him? Maybe he got to know you so that you would invite him to the party so he could pick us off one by one." Raegan said, getting into Claire's face this time.

"What? That's ridiculous!" Claire said while looking at Mick. She didn't want to believe the accusations, but defending Mick was getting harder and harder. Derek stepped forward; he'd heard enough.

"I don't know if you're guilty or not, but I'm not taking any chances." Derek grabbed a chair, brought it over and forced Mick to sit down. "Right now, you're our prime suspect."

"I've never met any of you before tonight; why would I want to kill you?" Mick said while Marco and Jack held him down in the chair. Derek grabbed a sheet of the bed and ripped it into strips. He then started tying Mick to the chair.

"So you're just going to leave me here tied to a chair next to a dead body?" Mick's tough guy exterior was starting to crack.

"Yes," Dereck said very matter-of-factly.

Everyone started to file out of the room, leaving Mick and Derek inside. "I haven't done anything; you can't do this," Mick said, pleading with Derek.

"Sorry, Mick, but right now, we don't have a choice. We'll be back when we know more." Derek left the room and closed the door behind him, leaving Mick alone in the room with Lin's body.

"You can't leave me here! I'm not the murderer!" Mick called Frantically from behind the door, but the others completely tuned him out.

Derek moved down the hall a bit, away from the room that Mick was tied up in. "We have to find the phones." He said in a loud whisper.

"Should we try the gate again?" Layla asked somewhat nervously. Before Derek could even answer, a loud crack of thunder ripped through the air.

"I think we have to wait for the weather to improve. Besides, it seems like opening the gate probably isn't going to happen anyways."

"You goddamn assholes! You can't leave me here!" Mick called from inside the room. Derek motioned for everyone to go downstairs. The group filed down the stairs leaving the upstairs eerily empty. They headed into the parlour to discuss their resumed search for the phones.

"I'll be there in a second; I need to go the washroom; I've been holding it for hours," Layla said, breaking away from the group and heading down the hall.

"I'm going to grab a drink of water; I don't trust anything I don't see come out of the faucet," Bryce said, leaving the group and heading to the kitchen. The rest of the group headed into the parlour.

Meanwhile, upstairs Mick continued to struggle, trying to free himself from the shabbily made bedsheet ropes.

"Hey! Get your asses back up here and untie me! You can't leave me like this!" Mick shook and struggled in the chair. He was struggling so hard that he almost missed the creak of the door opening. Mick looked up and saw a very surprising figure standing there in front of him.

"What? Where the hell did you come from?" Mick said to the figure looming over him.

"Are you here to untie me? Well, hurry up!" Mick said, assuming the figure was there to help him. Unfortunately, that wasn't the case. As the mysterious person moved closer, Mick clearly realized they weren't there to help him.

"Whoa. What's going on? I had nothing to do with any of this. Wait! Wait!"

There was a loud thud that everyone else would have easily heard if they weren't so busy arguing downstairs. Mick lay on the floor, still tied to the chair, as the figure slowly and quietly left the room unseen.

Chapter 11
THE PHONE

Everyone was now in the parlour, ready to discuss a plan. Claire, Michelle, Marco, Jack and Kara all sat down while Brook, Bryce, Layla, Derek and Raegan paced around the room. Everyone was talking over each other in an attempt to get themselves heard. They had reached the point in the night where they were so exhausted and scared that they were getting hyper. Finally, Raegan said something that cut through the noise.

"At least we have the murderer locked up." She said as everyone else fell silent. There were a lot of nods of agreement and murmurs of ya, and thank god. But Claire wasn't having it.

"Mick is not the murderer. He's not. And now he's alone and tied up next to a dead body. You're all monsters!" Claire was working hard to hold back her sobs. Layla walked over and put a hand on Claire's shoulder, but she quickly pulled it away. She didn't want comfort from anyone who believed Mick was responsible for this.

Finally, Jack decided to ask the question on everyone's mind, "What makes you think he's innocent? You yourself said you barely even know the guy." Claire glared at Jack; she didn't appreciate what he was insinuating.

"I know him well enough to know he's not a murderer." Claire rebutted as she got up from where she was sitting and walked to the furthest corner of the room.

"I mean, do you really? His note did say that he wasn't who he said he was; maybe you don't know him as well as you think." Brook said, trying to sound supportive when in actuality, she wanted to remind everyone of what his note said.

"Really? You should be one to talk! Didn't you just learn like half an hour ago that your husband had to basically change his identity after beating up his last girlfriend?" Claire and Brook were now in each other's faces, and things were escalating fast.

Derek decided he needed to chime in before things got any further off the rails. "Ok! Ok! Everybody calm the hell down. We can't start turning on each other. We are literally dropping like flies. Right now, Mick is our most likely suspect and since he's locked up, let's take the opportunity and search for the phones again. If we can find them, we can call for help and get the hell outta here. Agreed?" Derek looked around the room, and everyone nodded in agreement, even Claire.

"Ok, we will split into three groups, and this time we need to stick with our groups; no one goes off on their own. Claire, Raegan, Layla, Jack, you guys take the basement. Michelle, Brook, and Marco, you take this floor and start with the family room; that's where the box was last seen. Bryce, Kara and I will head upstairs." Derek didn't even ask if everyone agreed this time; he just gave the order.

As Claire, Raegan, Layla and Jack made their way into the basement, Claire started to sob softly, she was trying her best to hold it back, but her emotions were getting the best of her. Once they got into the basement, they made their way to the sitting room; all of their notes were sitting on the table, still exposing all of their secrets. Claire suddenly couldn't take it anymore and picked up a lamp and threw it to the ground, breaking it.

"Seriously, what the hell is going on? Why is someone killing all of us, and why does everyone think it's Mick? He doesn't even know any of you! He didn't even want to come!" Claire slumped on the ground next to the lamp she had just smashed and started ugly crying.

Layla decided to try again to comfort Claire, and this time she was much more receptive to it. Layla sat down beside Claire and placed a hand on her shoulder, and this time, rather than moving away, she turned and hugged Layla, crying into her shoulder.

"Maybe Mick is innocent, but right now, he's our best guess. If he didn't do it, then his name will be cleared, and he will get a heartfelt apology from each and every one of us." Layla knew the last part was a stretch, but since she thought Mick was guilty, it wouldn't matter.

Claire started to calm down a bit. Raegan came over and sat on the other side of her for a little added support. "The best way for us to clear Mick's name is to find the phones and call for help. We can leave it to the cops to figure out what happened and who is responsible." Raegan said, standing back up and helping Claire to her feet.

As Raegan, Layla and Claire got up from where they'd been sitting, they noticed Jack using his foot to hide the pieces of the broken lamp under the couch.

"What are you doing?" Claire asked Jack, her tears starting to transition to giggles.

"I. I'm not sure. I guess I didn't want the homeowner to see the broken lamp." Jack said, starting to laugh at himself. Suddenly, Raegan, Claire and Layla started laughing too. It was such a silly thing, but in the moment, it was the best thing that could have possibly happened.

It took about 5 minutes for the group to regain their composure and start looking for the box again. It was amazing how much-renewed hope comes from just a few minutes of laughter.

Upstairs in the family room, Marco threw a blanket over Anders' body as the group started looking for the phones. It was clear that everyone was really feeling the tension as they searched for the box of phones where it had originally been left.

"This is pointless! We've already searched the house for the phones. They're gone!" Marco said as he once again checked under the couch cushions.

"Do you have a better idea?" Michelle said, filled with rage. Neither Brook nor Marco had anything helpful to say.

Instead, Marco decided to berate the same point, "No. But that doesn't mean this plan isn't pointless." Marco tossed the pillow he'd been holding on the floor.

Brook had had enough of Marco's attitude. "Enough! Would you rather just sit and do nothing? Would you rather just wait around for the killer to knock us off one by one? We might as well keep looking. Even if we don't find the box of phones, we are keeping the killer on their toes by moving around the house in groups, and the owner will be back in the morning. It'll all be ok." Brook was pretty proud of her little motivational speech, but Marco wasn't feeling it.

"How can you be so positive? Our friends and our loved ones are literally dropping dead. Someone is marked to be next and is probably losing their mind right now." Marco said before remembering who was next in line.

"Not someone. Me. I'm the one losing my mind right now, knowing that at any moment, I could be dead. If we don't find a way out of here or a way to call for help soon, I'm gonna die!" Michelle yelled at the top of her lungs, right into Marco's face. Silence. Both Marco and Brook had no idea how to react to anything Michelle had just said.

"That's what I thought. Can we please keep looking?" Michelle walked away from the others and went back to searching. Marco and Brook silently joined her.

Derek, Bryce and Kara were searching the bedroom next to where Mick was tied up. "God, it's a total mess in here; how are we supposed to find anything?" Kara said, trying to search in the closet that was absolutely full of stuff.

"You know, Mick is the one that made this mess. He's the one who absolutely destroyed these bedrooms last time we searched, remember?" Kara said to Bryce and Derek.

"Do you think he was trying to cover up the fact the box is up here by messing the rooms so bad they are nearly impossible to search?" Bryce asked while moving the mattress out of the way.

"Probably. HEY MICK! WHERE'S THE BOX?" Derek shouted through the wall to Mick in the next room. Silence.

"It's kinda weird that Mick isn't yelling at us, isn't it?" Kara said to Derek and Bryce.

"I'm enjoying the silence. We can go check on him after we finish searching this room." Derek said as he started sifting through another pile of crap.

As Kara, Bryce, and Derek searched the room, the silence was deafening. None of them said a single word in favour of getting the job over with as quickly as possible. Kara was almost through everything in the closet when something caught her attention.

Ding.

It was very faint, but it sounded like a phone getting a text. She assumed it was just her mind playing tricks on her, it was the middle of the night after all, but then she heard it again.

Ding.

"Did you guys hear that?" Kara asked, sticking her head out of the closet.

"Hear what?" Marco asked, not even looking up from what he was going.

"The ding. There was a ding, like a phone getting a text. Just listen for a second." Kara had now gotten both Derek's and Bryce's attention. The three of them stood in total silence for a minute or two before giving up.

"Kara, are you sure you heard a phone dinging? Maybe it was just your imagination. Where were you when you heard it?" Derek asked, getting up from where he'd been searching.

"Here, I was in the closet when I heard the ding both times and there definitely isn't any phone in here. I've searched every inch of this closet." Derek and Bryce joined Kara in the closet, and the three stood in silence again.

Ding.

There it was again, it was very faint, but it was a phone dinging.

"Did you hear that? That was definitely a phone dinging!" Kara said excitedly.

"Yes. I heard it; what's next to this closet?" Bryce asked, putting his ear to the wall.

"The room that Mick's locked in, he must have a phone!" Derek was the first one out of the door, with Kara and Bryce right behind him.

Derek opened the door to the room where Mick was tied inside, and there, on the ground, still tied to the chair, was Mick. Kara and Bryce looked over his shoulder to see what was going on.

"On my god! You have got to be kidding me!" Kara said, stepping around Derek to take a better look. There was a small pool of blood next to Mick's head, and he wasn't moving at all.

"Is he dead?" Bryce asked, kicking Mick's foot; no reaction.

"This doesn't make any sense! Mick is the murderer; we were sure of it! He was number 16!" Kara said, feeling very vulnerable again. Derek was leaning in to get a closer look at Mick when he saw his crumpled-up note on the ground where he'd thrown it. Derek picked up the note and noticed that the one had been crossed out. Instead of 16, the note now said 6.

Ding.

The phone went off again, and this time it was loud; it had to be in the room with Mick. "I think the phone is on Mick. He had a phone all along!" Bryce said, starting to go through Mick's pockets.

"Got it!" He said, grabbing the phone out of Mick's inside pocket.

"Can you believe he had a phone the entire time? What an asshole!" Derek said, taking the phone from Bryce's hand.

"Damn! Look at the battery; it's about to die." Derek quickly scrolled through the notifications on the lock screen; they were all from someone named 'Boss,' but there were no message previews.

"Can you unlock it?" Kara asked frantically. Derek tried, but of course, it needed a passcode.

"Use his face, use his face!" Kara said frantically. Derek put the phone in front of Mick's face, but nothing happened.

"I can't get a good angle; we need to sit him up," Derek said, handing the phone to Kara.

Bryce and Derek heaved Mick back upright in the chair he was still tied to, and Kara turned to the phone towards Mick's face to unlock it.

"It's not working; we need his eyes to be open!" Before they could do anything else, the phone died.
Dead.

"It died! It died!" Kara said, frantically looking at Derek and Bryce.

"God damn it!" Bryce grabbed the phone from Kara's hands and whipped it against the wall, breaking it.

"Bryce! What the hell? Why would you do that?" Derek ran over and picked the phone up off the ground, but there was no saving it.

"Why would you break the only phone we had? What were you thinking? We could have charged it and used it to call for help!"

Bryce went white as a sheet; he never even thought about charging the phone. Derek picked up the broken phone and brought it to where Kara and Bryce were just as the others arrived upstairs.

"What's going on? We heard a bunch of commotion." Jack said, entering the room.

"Oh my god!" Claire said, seeing Mick slumped over in the chair.

"How could you?" She ran over to check on Mick while the others stood there, shocked.

Chapter 12
THE NEW SUSPECT

Claire wrapped her arms around Mick while glaring at Derek, Bryce and Kara. "We had nothing to do with it! We were searching the room next door when we heard a phone dinging, so we came in to look for it and found Mick like this." Kara said defensively.

"Wait, you found a phone?" Brook asked, completely skipping over the fact that Mick was dead.

"Yes, we found a phone, but it's useless now," Bryce said, trying to preemptively move the conversation along before anyone else found out why it was useless.

"What do you mean it's useless? I don't understand." Brook said, pressing the issue.

"It's useless because when it died, Bryce thought it would be a good idea to whip it against the wall rather than plug it in and charge it," Kara said happily throwing Bryce under the bus.

"Why did you break it? Did you not want us to be able to make a phone call?" Michelle asked, all but accusing him of having something to hide.

"What? No. I was just upset, and I wasn't thinking clearly." Bryce said, getting up in Michelle's face.

"I think you're whole abuse story is coming into sharper focus, isn't it, Bryce," Jack said before immediately regretting it. Bryce lunged at Jack, and it took Marco, Derek and Brook to break them up.

"Guys! Guys!" Layla yelled, trying to break through the ruckus.

"I think we're missing the bigger point here. Mick had a phone this entire time, and he said nothing! We could have called for help and been out of here hours ago!" Layla was right; if Mick wasn't the murderer, he was still responsible for at least some of the deaths. He could have helped, and he did nothing.

"It's because he's the murderer!" Brook said, feeling like she'd come up with some amazing revelation. Suddenly it hit her why that probably isn't the case.

"Ok, well, he's still guilty of something…I haven't taken my nightly painkillers. Things are a little fuzzy." Brook sat down on the mattress that was now on the floor and put her head in her hands.

"Wait, how did you find the phone again? You heard it dinging?" Layla said to Kara, Bryce and Derek.

"Ya, that's right," Kara replied.

"Did you check the notifications?" Layla asked, getting more and more anxious.

"Yes, they were from someone called Boss, but we didn't see any of the messages, only the notifications, and then the phone died and then someone broke it," Derek said, glaring at Bryce.

"What? The notifications were from 'Boss' are you serious? He must have been working with the killer!" Layla said, starting to piece things together.

"But none of us had ever met him tonight other than…Claire." Marco said, looking to Claire, who was still over near Mick's body.

"Are you kidding me? Now I'm a suspect? You know me! How could you think I had anything to do with this?" Claire said, backing away from Mick's body towards the door.

"Sorry Claire, but right now, you're our prime suspect," Derek said, getting between Claire and the door.

"Search me! If you were hearing dings, then the person texting them would have a phone on them." Claire patted herself down and turned out her pockets; no phone.

"You could have ditched it somewhere. Someone was texting Mick, and right now, you're our best guess." Derek said, feeling slightly less convinced of Claire's guilt.

"Well, so far, you haven't been great at picking your suspects, and all of your suspects have wound up dead!" Claire said, trying to somehow get around Derek and make a run for it. Marco and Bryce stepped in the way, and Claire was totally trapped.

"You're right; leaving suspects alone hasn't worked well. So instead you aren't allowed to leave the group. Understand?" Derek said, looking Claire straight in the eye. Claire nodded her head in agreement; no point trying to argue.

"Ok, can we do the rest of this somewhere else? Like not in a room with two dead bodies." Brook said, making her way toward the door.

"Good idea; I need to get out of here," Kara said, joining Brook.

"Let's head to the parlour," Jack said, heading to the door while trying to steer clear of Bryce.

Jack lead the way downstairs to the parlour, with everyone following behind me. Claire walked between Derek and Marco; she wasn't going anywhere, not that there was anywhere to go. Once everyone was in the room, Layla got right down to business. "So what now? Who has number 6?" Layla asked, looking around the room.

Michelle put her hand up, "I do." She said shakily. "And I have number five," Kara added. "Lin's number was changed to 5, and Mick's was changed to six. Does that me you guys got skipped?" Layla asked, looking to Claire for an answer. "I have no idea! I had nothing to do with any of this." Claire said, practically in tears.

"Ok, well, if we assume that Kara and Michelle are skipped, that means that…." Layla was about to say who was next, but Raegan did it for her, "I'm next." Layla tried to make her feel better, but even she didn't believe what she was saying, "Well, there's no way you're dying! We are going to figure out what's going on before anyone else dies."

"So what do we do now? Back to looking for the phones?" Marco said, looking around the room. There was a collective groan. "Hold on!" Bryce said, popping out of his chair, "With everything going on,

Brook and I forgot to tell you what we found. "Oh ya!" Brook said, cutting in, "When we were searching the fence for any openings, we saw a light in the distance like someone with a flashlight and a narrow opening in the fence right behind the back door, the one in the kitchen." Brook said excitedly.

"Oh my god, what? Why didn't you say anything sooner?" Derek said frantically.

"We did mention it didn't we I think we did. Ugh, I'm so fuzzy right now," Brook said, getting up.

"But I think it's worth checking out, right?" Brook headed for the parlour door, and everyone followed behind her.

Layla and Raegan were the last ones left in the room. "Nothing is going to happen to you, I promise," Layla said, hugging Raegan tight.

"How could you possibly know that? I'm next! I'm about to die! Oh god, how is this happening? What did I do to deserve this? What did any of us do to deserve this?" Raegan and Layla hugged for a long moment as Layla tried to reassure her.

"You're not going to die. I promise." Layla said, holding Raegan tight.

After another moment, Layla and Raegan separated. Layla grabbed Raegan's hand, and the two of them went to find the others in the kitchen.

When the group arrived in the kitchen, the first thing they did was check the backdoor.

"It's unlocked," Marco said, opening the backdoor easily.

"That's what Lin was going to tell me when she found Anders and I together; she'd found the back door unlocked," Kara added, suddenly remembering the moment that Lin found her and Anders.

"There, back there. That's where the opening is in the fence." Bryce said, stepping outside. The rain had died down enough that they could go outside without getting completely drenched.

"Kara, can you come with us? The opening in the fence is really narrow, and I think you're the only one of us with any chance of getting through." Bryce said to a very nervous Kara.

Kara looked outside. It was so dark, and the fence wasn't exactly close to the house; the backyard was massive. Kara looked at the group, "Is anyone else coming with me?" She asked nervously.

"Ya, I'll go with you," Bryce replied.

"Me too," Brook added.

"And me," Marco said. Kara nodded yes, and the four of them stepped out the backdoor and into the backyard.

Layla and Raegan arrived in the kitchen just as Bryce, Marco, Brook and Kara went out the backdoor.

"What's going on?" Layla asked, seeing everyone looking out the backdoor.

"The backdoor was unlocked, and there's a small opening in the fence. They went to see if Kara could fit through it." Derek said, filling Layla and Raegan in.

"Wait, if the rain stopped, should we try the gate again?" Jack asked with a new sense of hope.

"Yes! Great idea!." Derek said, starting towards the front door.

"Wait. The gate is useless; the security is like nothing I've ever seen before; there's no way you're going to get it open with a code." Raegan said, reminding everyone of her expertise.

"It's worth a shot!" Derek said. "Who's coming with me?" Jack, Michelle and Claire all put their hands up, I mean, Claire didn't want to, but she also didn't want to separate from the group.

"Michelle, are you sure you want to go out there?" Derek said nervously.

Michelle nodded her head yes. "I'll be ok, thanks."

"We'll keep looking for the phones," Layla said to the group pointing to Raegan and herself.

"Ok, be careful," Derek said as he and the group left the kitchen. Once again, everyone was split up, which never seemed to end well.

Chapter 13

THE BODY

Layla looked to Raegan, "I have an idea; I think I know where the phones are. We never checked for an attic." Layla said with eyes lighting up.

"Oh my god, you're right! There must be an attic somewhere; let's go!" Raegan grabbed Layla's hand, and the two of them ran up the stairs.

"We should check the main bedroom closet; I bet that's where it is," Layla said, leading the way down the hall.

Raegan and Layla walked into the large bedroom at the back of the house and into the closet.

"There!" Layla said, pointing to a small loop handle hanging from the ceiling. Since Raegan was the taller of the two, she climbed up on the shelving and grabbed for the handle pulling down the door and extending the ladder.

Layla and Raegan climbed up the ladder and into the attic.

"Ugh, it's so dark up here, I can't see anything," Raegan said, grabbing for Layla's hand.

"Even if the phones are up here, we'll never be able to see them, and this attic is huge; how are we supposed to search this whole thing in the dark?" Layla said, feeling frustrated.

"I bet we can find a flashlight; I think we should go down and check," Raegan said, moving backward toward the ladder.

Raegan and Layla slowly climbed back down the ladder into the bedroom closet. Layla started walking out of the closet when Raegan had a thought.

"What if the killer isn't any of us? What if someone else is in the house? Raegan said nervously. Layla stopped and turned around to face Raegan.

"I mean, it's possible, but we've literally searched every inch of this house; if there were somewhere here, we would have seen them," Layla said, starting to walk again.

"Would we?" Raegan said not willing to give up on her idea. "This house is massive; there could easily be someone else here watching us from a distance and moving in the opposite direction as we are. It's not likely, but it's certainly possible." Raegan felt a chill rush down her spine at the thought of it. Layla grabbed Raegan's hand and led her out of the closet; they needed to find a flashlight and fast.

Kara, Marco, Brook and Bryce had finally reached the fence at the back of the property. "So, where's this opening you were talking about?" Kara asked nervously.

"It's right here," Bryce said, walking over to the spot with the small opening.

"Wow, that is really small; I don't think I can even fit through there." Kara took off her heavy sweatshirt and made her way to the spot in the fence that she was supposed to go through. Kara turned her body to the side, sucked in as much as possible, and attempted to squeeze herself through. She got one leg through with no problem, but when it came to her torso, there was no way she was going through.

"I can't fit, guys. I honestly don't think there's any way an adult could get through this opening. Maybe a child, but definitely no one over the age of 12." Kara pulled her leg back out and stepped away from the fence.

Everyone looked deflated. Here was yet another dead end. Kara, Bryce, Brook and Marco made their way back to the house in hopes that the rest of the group had made some progress.

Derek, Claire, Jack and Michelle walked out the front door and headed toward the gate. As they started to get closer to the gate, Michelle started to visibly tense up.

"You can go back to the house; you don't have to come," Claire said to Michelle putting her hand on her shoulder.

"Will you come with me?" Michelle said to Claire starting the tear up.

"Of course." She replied. As Claire and Michelle made their way towards Asher's body Jack and Derek walked towards the gate to see if they could make any progress opening it.

As Michelle and Claire got closer to where Asher died, Michelle felt a chill run down her spine.

"Asher, Asher's gone," Michelle said with a very shaky voice.

"I know, hun, and it's heartbreaking; he was such a great guy," Claire said, attempting to comfort Michelle.

"No, he's gone! His body's gone! He was right there." Michelle screamed as if she herself was being murdered, causing Derek and Jack to run over and check on her.

"Michelle! Are you ok? What's going on?" Derek ran full speed over to Michelle and pulled Claire away from her.

"No, no, it wasn't Claire. It's Asher; he's gone!" Derek looked over to where Asher's body had been lying, and Michelle was right; he was nowhere to be seen.

"What? How? I don't understand." Derek was as dumbfounded as Michelle.

"Did anyone check his pulse? Did anyone actually confirm he was dead?" Jack asked frantically.

"No. Right after he died, the storm started, and we all ran inside. But he was dead; I watched him die." Michelle said, sobbing.

"How could someone steal his body?" Michelle was starting to spiral out of control.

"Maybe he wasn't dead," Jack said.

"Maybe Asher is the murderer," Claire said, continuing Jack's thought.

"How could you say something like that? I watched Asher die. He died in my arms." Michelle said, getting into Claire's face. Derek gently put a hand on Michelle, holding her back.

"You have to admit it's a little strange that someone would steal Asher's body. None of the other bodies were moved. Were they?" Claire said, looking to Jack and Derek for confirmation.

"No, I don't think any of the other bodies were moved but we haven't actually checked. In fact, we haven't really checked the rooms where bodies were left other than the family room and Lin's body in the bedroom." Derek said, starting to question everything he'd seen.

"And you were skipped!" Claire said with a sudden realization.

"You were supposed to be the next to die, but Mick died instead! It wasn't me that was in on it; it was you!" Claire said, backing away from Michelle. "We don't even know if that was Mick's phone that was found, maybe it was Asher's, and he planted it on Mick to throw everyone off."

Jack, Claire and Derek started to back away from Michelle. "What is happening? My husband was murdered, his body was stolen, and now you're accusing me of what? Being a murderer? Or an accomplice to murder? How could you?!" Michelle started crying her eyes out. Every aspect of her life had disintegrated in a matter of hours, and she was beginning to lose her grip on reality.

"We need to get back inside and tell the others what's going on, and we should check that all of the other bodies are still where we left them, which I hope to god they are," Jack said, starting to jog back towards the door. Claire, Derek and Michelle followed behind him on their way back into the house.

As Jack opened the front door, he saw Raegan and Layla come down from upstairs and Bryce, Brook, Marco and Kara come in from the kitchen.

"We've got news!" Layla, Jack and Bryce all said at the same time. The group once again made their way into the parlour to try and get a handle on everything that was going on.

Chapter 14

THE NEWS

"I can't believe we're back in this room again! I want to go home." Brook said, slumping into her usual spot. As everyone filed into the room, ready to share their news, Michelle was visibly shaken.

"Ok, so we made a shocking discovery out front.." Derek said, leaning on the window at the front of the room.

He was about to finish his thought when Michelle chimed in, "Asher is gone!" Everyone who didn't know what she was referring to gave Michelle a sympathetic look.

"Not dead but gone; his body's gone," Derek said, clarifying Michelle's dramatic statement.

"What? What do you mean?" Raegan said, popping up from her chair.

"When we went outside to look for a way to open the gate, we noticed that Asher's body was gone, which means one of two things. Someone moved his body or..." Jack was trying to sound sympathetic, but he definitely believed.

"Asher's the murderer!" Raegan said, finishing Jack's thought.

Michelle was, of course, quick to defend him once again. "Asher is not the murderer! He is a victim! Someone moved his body! We have to find him!" Michelle looked around the room for support but couldn't find a single sympathetic face. She slumped down and started sobbing. Layla offered her a pat on the back, but it wasn't particularly heartfelt.

"So, that's what happened out front. Bryce, what happened out back?" Derek said, moving the conversation along.

"Well, we made it to the opening in the fence, and Kara attempted to go through, but even she couldn't fit. So if Kara couldn't fit, there is no way someone used the opening to get in or out of the house." Bryce finished and sat down. Everyone looked at him, a little disappointed. All of them had secretly hoped the killer had escaped out of the back and they were safe.

"Wait, someone used the code to enter the house around the time the box was dropped off. Did I mention that already? I can't keep track of everything! But someone was here, opened the gate and then locked the gate; I have no idea which side of it they were on when they locked it, though." Raegan said, recalling what she had found earlier in the evening.

The group all sat with blank stares. Could this night get any worse?

"So we think the box of phones might be in the attic." Layla piped in, getting everyone's attention.

"I mean, we don't know for sure because it's pitch black up there, but it seems like a definite possibility. With a flashlight, we would be able to know for sure." Layla finished and looked around the room to see a renewed hope in everyone's eyes, finally, some good news.

"Ok, so let's find a flashlight! There's probably one in the…."Derek was just about to say kitchen when a door slammed.

"Did you hear that?" Marco said, interrupting Derek.

"Of course we heard that!" Brook shouted! Raegan looked around the room and did a quick head count; everyone was accounted for.

"We're all here, so it's either someone from outside or Asher," Raegan said, looking in Michelle's direction. Another door slammed. Someone is looking for something.

Marco had had enough talking; time to do something. He stood up and was about to leave the parlour when Jack got in his way.

"Cool it for a second. Do you really want to come face to face with a murderer without a weapon or a plan?" Jack said, trying to slow Marco. Without another word, Marco pushed past Jack, left the parlour, and ran up the stairs. Jack instinctively followed him even though he didn't think it was a great move. The rest of the group was less enthusiastic but eventually made their way up the stairs.

Marco went to the left, and Jack went to the right; they started at the back of the house, opening bedroom doors and looking inside.

"This one's empty." Jack said after searching the first bedroom.

"This one too," Marco said from the other side of the hall.

"Empty," Jack said from the next bedroom.

"Ditto," Marco said, moving to the next room.

"Here too," Jack added.

"No one in here," Marco said.

Jack got to the last door on his side of the hall and opened it, it was the room with Mick and Lin's bodies, but there was one problem.

"It's gone?" Jack yelled, drawing everyone's attention. Derek was, of course, the first one there.

"What's gone?" He asked, bursting into the room. Jack, didn't even need to answer. As soon as Derek set foot into the room, it was obvious what was gone. Mick was gone.

"What? What the hell is happening?" Derek said, losing his normally calm demeanour. Claire looked around Derek to see what was going on.

"Someone stole Mick's body!" Claire said with a scream.

"Or he wasn't actually dead, and he's our killer!" Kara said while checking to ensure Lin was still where they left her.

"He and Asher must be working together; it's the only explanation that makes sense!" Derek said, starting to wrap his head around the situation.

"Mick never even met Asher before tonight! Why would he be helping Asher murder everyone?" Claire said, yelling at Derek.

"Why would Asher want to kill anyone? Especially his sister? He loved Amy!" Michelle yelled at Claire. Suddenly Derek's world became clear; he knew what was going on.

"The inheritance!" Derek said with a sudden epiphany. He was just about to elaborate when there was another door slam. The group went silent, listening to hear if they could tell where that was coming from.

"Why did you run upstairs when the door slammed the first time?" Layla said to Marco.

"What do you mean? I heard the doors slam and ran upstairs to see what was going on." Marco replied, not appreciating the insinuation.

"But why upstairs? There are doors on every floor of this house; why did you immediately assume it came from upstairs?" Layla seemed to be leading somewhere, and everyone just let her keep going.

"Why not? I didn't tell everyone to follow me. You could have chosen to check another floor. I just assumed the door slamming was upstairs." Marco said, pushing past Layla and heading for the stairs again.

The group made their way back to the parlour; it had definitely become their safe space. As they all made their way inside, Raegan asked the question that everyone had been wondering, "Ok, tell us about this inheritance. What happened?" Raegan said, pressing Derek to continue his story.

Derek took a deep breath and then explained what had gone on.

"When Amy and Asher's parents died in the car accident a few months ago, there were some hard feelings about how things were left in the will." Michelle scoffed, "That's putting it mildly!" She added with disdain. "Ya, it was a little more than just hard feelings. Amy and Asher actually hadn't spoken since the will was read, that I know of. That's why I was so surprised to see him here tonight. You see, Amy's parents were quite wealthy, and she was left 80% of the money and Asher was only left 20%. They had both assumed it would be a 50/50 split and it wasn't. Asher contested the will right away. The ruling is due to come out any day now." Derek looked to Michelle to see her reaction; she looked away, refusing to make eye contact with him.

"That's how we afforded our big new house and our new cars and even to host this ridiculous birthday party. Even though Amy hasn't gotten the money yet, the lawyer told her that it looked like she would end up with what was originally in the will. Amy has just been spending money like we have a never-ending stream, and I think Asher couldn't handle it. " The words poured out of Derek as his brain continued putting the puzzle together.

"This is ridiculous! Are you implying that Asher murdered Amy, his little sister, to get more of the inheritance? That doesn't even make sense! And what would his motive be to murder everyone else?" Michelle was getting very defensive. She picked up a vase and threw it at the wall, narrowly missing Layla.

"Whoa! Ok, maybe cool it a bit, Michelle." Layla said, moving away from the broken vase. Michelle rushed out of the room sobbing as Raegan followed behind her trying to slow her down.

Everyone else turned to see what else Derek had to say. "I'm sure she'll cool off in a minute. I mean, with everything that's come to light, it seems like Asher is the murderer; he has to be."

"And Mick. They must have been working together. It makes sense that Asher was the one messaging him. Once the rain started, we just left him out there. He could have easily gotten back into the house, gotten the phones without any of us ever suspecting him." Kara said, continuing to wade through all of the things that had happened that evening.

"I still feel like Mick's innocent," Claire added in quietly.

"Really? With everything going on, how could you still think he's innocent?" Brook asked, shocked.

"Well, I do!" Claire said, standing up.

"There's no way!" Brook replied. The room erupted into yells and screams, with everyone letting out all of the stress and anger that they had been holding in for the entire evening.

The noise in the parlour grew and grew until a loud, sharp noise broke through the air.

Bang.

Bang.

Two gunshots cut through the air, one after the other. The group was motionless, paralyzed with fear. They waited for a long moment to see if there would be another gunshot, but there was only silence.

Finally, Claire decided to say something, "Where are Michelle and Raegan?" She asked with a shaky voice.

"Raegan!" yelled Layla, suddenly snapping out of her daze. Layla ran out of the parlour and into the hall, followed by the rest of the group.

"Raegan! Raegan!" Layla yelled frantically. "Raegan, please answer me!" Still no answer.

As Layla stood frozen, yelling Raegan's name, Derek made his way down the hall to see if he could find them. The first room he came to was the library. He poked his head inside, and it was gruesome. There, lying dead on the library floor, were Raegan and Michelle. Each of them held a gun in their hand.

Layla noticed Derek standing motionless in the doorway; she already knew what he had found. She rushed over to see for herself and immediately wished she hadn't. Layla pushed past Derek and ran to Raegan's motionless body, picking her up and cradling her in her arms.

Bryce was standing next to Derek, both of them in total shock, but what they saw before them. "How the hell did this happen? It looks like they shot each other. Why did they shoot each other?" Bryce asked Derek, knowing full well he had no answer to give.

Derek and Bryce stepped further into the room to get a closer look at what had happened as Claire, Jack, Brook, Kara and Marco followed behind. Brook went right over to Layla and pried her away from Raegan's body, pulling her into a hug.

"I don't understand. Why did they shoot each other? It doesn't make any sense!" Layla said through sobbing tears.

"It's sad, isn't it?" That voice. It couldn't be, but it was. Everyone turned around to see Asher standing there in the doorway, very much alive.

Now to understand how we got this point, we need to go back six months to the will reading for Mr. and Mrs. Rawling.

Amy and Derek entered the lawyer's office to see Asher and Michelle already there. Asher got up and hugged Amy, "How you holding up, Aim?" He said, holding his sister tight. Amy hugged Asher; she was so glad to have her big brother with her. As Amy and Derek found their seats, the lawyer entered the office and closed the door behind her.

"Mr. and Mrs. Rawlings, Mr. and Mrs. Sumner." She said, greeting the couples and taking her seat.

"Thank you for coming in today. For starters, I would like to offer all of you my deepest condolences. Losing both of your parents at such a young age and so tragically must have been incredibly difficult." The lawyer looked at the two couples with sympathy.

"Reading a will is never easy, and it is even more difficult in cases like this." The lawyer opened the file on her desk and looked down at the document. "Usually, in the case of siblings, the will is split evenly between them, but in the case of Mr. and Mrs. Rawlings, your parents, that wasn't the case." The lawyer picked up a sticky note from the document and moved it to the side.

"As I'm sure you both know, your parents had amassed a great deal of wealth in their lifetime, especially when you take all of their assets into account. The total that was left behind was," the lawyer looked at her sticky note to make sure she had the correct amount, "10.2 million." The lawyer paused for a moment and looked at Amy and Asher, who were both working hard to hide the smiles that had appeared on their faces.

"Now, here's where it gets tricky. As I mentioned above, most parents split the money evenly between their children, but that wasn't the case with your parents. Now I want to assure you that I have read through every page in detail multiple times to ensure I was correct, and according to your parents' wishes, Amy will receive 80% of the inheritance, and Asher will receive 20% of the inheritance totalling 8.16 million and 2.04 million respectively." The lawyer finished speaking and paused to give the siblings a moment to digest what they had just heard.

Amy turned to Derek and hugged him; 8.16 million, they were set for life! Asher, on the other hand, had a far less favourable reaction.

"What?! I don't? I can't? Are you sure? How could they do this to me?" Asher asked, putting his head in his hands. Michelle reached over to rub Asher's back, but he moved away.

"There was more context included in the will, but I wasn't sure if that was something you wanted read aloud." The lawyer said, handing Asher a copy of the will.

"To our son Asher, we leave 20% of our worldly possessions. We have seen him struggle with money over the years and feel that leaving him too much would only burden him further, and we want him to live a happy and full life free from the added stress of wealth…." Asher put the will back down on the desk.

"Are you kidding me? They don't want to burden me with more money? They think giving Amy four times the amount they left me will be less of a burden!" Asher stood up from his chair and started pacing around the room.

"What can I do about this? There must be something I can do about this. Is there not some legal recourse I can use to object to this abomination?" Asher shoved his chair backwards in frustration as Michelle quietly picked it back up.

"Mr. Rawlings, I understand what kind of shock news like this can bring, and you are well within your right to contest the will and…." The lawyer didn't even finish getting the statement out before Asher agreed.

"Yes, contest the will. I want to contest the will, I deserve 50%, not 20%, not 40% but 50%, and I will not rest until I get it." Asher said, slamming his hand down on the desk.

"Ok. I will start a motion to contest the will. On what grounds are you contesting?" The lawyer asked, getting out a piece of paper to take notes.

"What are the options?" Asher asked, sitting back down.

"Lack of capacity, undue influence, improper execution, fraud, ambiguity.." Asher stopped her there.

"Yes, that all of that, every single area," Asher said, putting his hands up.

"It will cost around $40,000 to contest the will." The lawyer said to Asher, who waved his hand for her to keep going. "And all of the assets will be frozen until everything is complete." The lawyer looked at Amy, who was glaring at her brother in disbelief.

Amy got up from her chair and walked over to Asher. "I will never forgive you for this. You're dead to me." Amy said, storming out of the office. Derek looked at the lawyer, then at Asher, then followed Amy into the hall.

Now that Amy and Derek were gone, Asher decided to ask the lawyer some honest questions. "So what are the odds I win this?" He asked her frankly.

"If you want my honest opinion. Not good. This will is well written, and your parents were clearly in their right state of mind when it was created." The lawyer said honestly. "And what happens if something were to happen to Amy while the will is still being contested?" Asher asked, making the lawyer nervous.

"Well, the way it is worded, the money would go to you, and if something happened to you, the money would go to Amy, and if something happened to both of you, it would go to your next closest relative." The lawyer said, ensuring she read all the options as she didn't love where this question was headed.

"Ok, thanks. I still want to go ahead with contesting the will." Asher said, putting on his coat.

The lawyer stood up to see them off, "I'll be in touch." She said before sitting and writing a sticky note, 'Asher Rawlings unstable?' she put the note on the front of the will and closed the envelope, not realizing the full ramifications of this conversation.

Chapter 16
THE PLAN

Asher was silent on the drive home. His mind raced at the possibility of inheriting the full 10.2 million dollars for himself. When he pulled into the driveway, he got out of the car and went right into the house, leaving a stunned and quite depressed Michelle alone with her thoughts. Asher grabbed his laptop, took it into the basement and closed the door. The basement was half-finished, one of the many jobs that Asher had started and abandoned. Asher walked over to the couch, pushed aside some clothes and sat down.

Asher opened his laptop and googled 'private investigators, Toronto.' This brought up lots of ads and some very shady-looking characters. Asher thought for a moment, then typed in, 'help locating family or friend, Toronto.' This search yielded some much better candidates. Asher scrolled through the names before landing on someone named 'Michael Patters.'

Asher clicked on Michael Patters' link and was taken to his website. He scanned through what it said, 'discreet' and 'no questions asked' and 'anonymous options available' and 'I will find out what you want to know' this guy was perfect, Asher thought to himself. Asher picked up his phone and texted the number on the website. 'Michael, I would like to hire you to do some investigating for me, but for various reasons, I need to remain anonymous. I will pay you upfront, and I will pay well. If you are interested, please reply yes.

Asher put his phone down and waited. He checked his phone, nothing. He went and worked out and checked his phone again, but still nothing.

"Ash, dinner time," Michelle called from upstairs. Asher grabbed his phone and was just heading upstairs when his phone buzzed. He looked at it and saw a reply. I'm interested. Tell me exactly what you need, and I will tell you my rate. What do I call you?' Asher smiled to himself; gotcha, he thought.

'Thanks, Michael. You can call me Boss.' Asher replied. Asher waited for a moment while Michael replied. 'Nice to meet you, Boss. You can call me Mick.'

Asher went upstairs to have his dinner, and Michelle couldn't help but comment on his change of attitude.

"You're in a much better mood." She said, clearing the plates from the table.

"Ya know, I had some time to reflect, and I'm feeling much better about the whole thing. If we end up getting more money, great. If we don't, so be it. I'm just glad I have you, and no amount of money will ever change that." Asher said, kissing Michelle on the cheek.

Michelle was just about to leave the kitchen when Asher called to her. "Oh, Michy, I know that you and Amy are close, and even though I'm fighting with her right now, you don't need to be." Michelle ran over and kissed Asher on the cheek.

"I'm so glad to hear you say that; I'm going to geo text her right now!" Michelle left the kitchen, and had she turned around, she would have seen the smile on Asher's face and immediately known he was up to something.

Over the next few weeks, Asher encouraged Michelle to keep in touch with Amy and would constantly ask Michelle what was happening in her life and how she was doing. Michelle took it as a sign that Asher was starting to come around when in fact, he was mining for information in an attempt to figure out who Amy's closest friends were. Anytime Michelle mentioned someone, he would text their name to Mick with instructions to find the deepest darkest secret he could about that person.

So far, Asher had sent Mick the names of himself, Michelle, Derek, Layla, Raegan, Brook and Bryce. He knew Amy was going to plan something big for her 35th birthday party and figured that she would invite this group at the least and probably others. In order for Asher's plan to work, he needed dirt, good dirt on every person who was going to be at her party.

As Amy's birthday loomed closer and closer, he planted the idea of having a big overnight bash into Michelle's head so she could, in turn, pass it on to Amy, which she did. He also found out a few more names of people Amy would likely invite, including Kara, Jack, Colleen, Mark, Lin and Anders.

Lucky for Asher, Mick wasn't just good at his job; he was great. Every day Asher would get an update on what he had discovered, and it didn't take long before he had a juicy piece of gossip on everyone. Now it was time for the hardest part, getting Michelle to convince Amy to invite them.

"Hey Michy, I know Amy's birthday is coming up soon, and I don't want to miss it. Do you think you could maybe plant the idea of inviting us?" Asher said, trying his best to sound like a sincere older brother.

"Oh my god, yes! She was just telling me that she wanted to have this 70s-themed murder mystery party, but she was short four people. I already told her to invite Claire and tell her to bring a date, but I will tell her we want to come too! I'm gonna text her right now."

As Michelle left to text Amy, Asher quickly messaged Mick, they had a late addition to the list, possibly two people. "Mick, I need to add another name to the list, Claire Rawlings." Asher watched as the typing bubble appeared, then disappeared,

appeared, then disappeared; it wasn't like Mick to be so indecisive. Finally, the message came through. 'I know her. We're dating.'

"Oh my god, yes! Yes!" Asher yelled out loud.

"What was that?" Michelle called from the other room.

"Nothing Michy, just playing a game," Asher replied, calming himself down. He started to reply to Mick.

'That's perfect. When she invites you to a 70s-themed birthday party, say yes.' There was no reply from Mick, but Asher knew he'd gotten the message. Now for the next part of his plan.

It took a few days, but Asher took the information he had learned from Mick and created notes for everyone attending the party, including himself. He then went through and numbered everyone being sure to put Amy first and Mick last. For his plan to work perfectly, the order was very important. As Asher was working away, Michelle burst into the room, startling him.

"We're invited!" She said, showing Asher the invitation from Amy.

"Amy's turning 35, and we are taking a trip back to the 70s! Join us on April 5th for the '70s-themed murder mystery party! Inside this envelope, you will find the details about your character and whether or not you're the murderer. Be sure to come dressed in costume and ready to party. The party will take place at 552 Walton Way, Coldwater, Ontario, and you are invited to stay the night." Asher read the invite and looked and Michelle, "Sounds fun." He said, passing the invitation back to her.

"So we can go?" She asked.

"We can go." He replied.

Michelle left the room all smiles and immediately messaged Amy to let her know they were coming. While Michelle contacted Amy, Asher looked up the address online and found it listed on Air BnB. He clicked on the listing and saw the homeowner's name, Courtney Krisp. Asher found her contact information and messaged her.

'Hi Courtney, I will be attending Amy Sumner's birthday party on April 5th at your home on

Walton Way, and I'm wondering if you could do me a favour. I want to surprise Amy with a big gift, but it needs to arrive mysteriously to go with her murder mystery theme. If I get the present to you ahead of time, would you be able to deliver it to the front door at 8 PM, ring the doorbell and then leave, so it looks like it mysteriously arrived? Also, I see the property has a big gate; could you be sure it is locked and secured before you go? Thanks for your help.'

Asher only had to wait a moment for a reply from Courtney, 'OMG, I love it. Yes, yes, yes!' Asher smiled to himself as he replied, 'thank you.' Everything was falling into place.

Chapter 17
THE EXECUTION

Finally, the day of the birthday party arrived. "Come on, Michy, we gotta go!" He called to Michelle as she came out of the house.

"I'm coming, I'm coming!" she said, running down the driveway. "How do I look?" She asked, showing off her outfit.

"Gorgeous as always," Asher said, giving Michelle a big kiss.

"Oh, Ashy! Don't ruin my makeup." She said with a giggle as she got into the car.

Once Michelle was in the car, Asher headed down to the basement for one more bag. "One sec!" He called as he ran back into the house. Asher quickly went to the basement to grab the bag with everything he needed for that night. He had two guns, some cyanide pills, and a box of Alka-seltzer.

Asher sent a quick text to Courtney, 'all ready to bring the package at 8?' and in true Courtney fashion, her reply was instant, 'you bet!'

Asher headed back upstairs and out to the car; he threw his bag in the trunk then hopped in the driver's seat.

"Sorry about that." Asher said as Michelle gave him 'the look.'

"And you say I'm slow." She said, full of attitude.

"Thanks for remembering my water bottle." He said, taking a big sip.

"Let's go!" Asher pulled out of the driveway, and they were off, ready for a party and whatever else the night might bring.

When Asher and Michelle pulled up to the gate, it opened automatically. Asher hoped that Courtney would remember to lock it after dropping off the package. Asher parked the car, and he and Michelle got out.

"You ready? It's been months since you've seen Amy." Michelle said, looking at Asher with concern.

"I'm ready. I'm looking forward to seeing my baby sister; I miss her." Asher added with a smile.

"Just promise me one thing, do not bring up the will or the money or anything to do with your parents tonight, deal?" Michelle said, looking Asher in the eye.

"Promise." He replied before giving her a kiss.

Asher went to the trunk and grabbed the two bags. He quickly removed two guns he had brought and placed them back in the trunk. He closed the trunk and brought the bags with him to the house. Asher rang the doorbell, and the two of them waited.

"Amy didn't tell anyone we were coming, just so you know." Michelle blurted out while they waited for the door to be answered. Asher was just about to reply when the door opened.

"Amy!" Michelle said, wrapping her arms around Amy.

"Hey Michelle, so glad you could make it." Michelle walked past Amy leaving Asher and Amy alone.

"Hey, Aim. How are you? It's been a while." Asher said, opening his arms for a hug.

"It has. I've missed you." Amy said, stepping into Asher's grip for a hug. After a moment, Amy pushed back and looked at her brother.

"Well, come in. Everyone's in the family room at the back of the house, and you can take your bag up to any of the empty rooms upstairs."

Asher grabbed the bags and went upstairs while Michelle and Amy chatted in the front hall. When Asher got to the top of the stairs, he opened the first door on the left, occupied. He continued opening doors until he found an empty room. Asher put their main bag on the bed and then put his other bag in the closet but not before removing the vile of cyanide and the candy that would cause the foaming mouth.

Asher closed the bedroom door and made his way downstairs, meeting Amy and Michelle in the hall.

"Shall we?" He said, putting his arms around Amy and Michelle's shoulders. When they arrived in the family room, everyone was shocked to see them, but none more shocked than Derek. Asher took a moment to look around the room, noting who was there and eventually, he found the person he was looking for, Mick. Mick still had no idea who he was, but Asher knew he would be integral to his plan.

Asher tried his best to visit with people so as not to draw suspicion to himself, but he couldn't help but keep checking the time. The package would be there soon, and they hadn't even started moving towards dinner. Finally the moment arrived, time to eat.

As everyone got in line to get themselves food, Asher noticed the backdoor in the kitchen. Perfect, he thought to himself. While everyone was busy serving themselves food and chatting, Asher nonchalantly walked over to the door and made it appear like he was looking out the window, then took the opportunity to unlock the back door.

Asher was the last to get in line to grab his food. While he waited his turn, he checked his watch, not long now. Once everyone had filled their plates, things moved quickly. Asher looked at his watch again, it was almost time, and that's when everything started to go off the rails. Asher looked over and saw that Kara was choking. Wow, he thought to himself, this is certainly setting the right mood. Just as Kara was recovering, the doorbell rang.

Asher was about to volunteer to answer the door, but Jack beat him to it. He hoped Courtney would be gone by the time he got there. When Jack returned a moment later with the box he certainly didn't act like he'd seen anyone at the door, things were still on.

Once everyone had opened their envelopes and read their notes, Asher nonchalantly scanned the room. He could tell by looking at their faces that the revelations had touched a nerve; Mick was worth every penny. Asher looked at Mick last and noticed the slightest change in his expression, perfect.

As everyone moved around the house, freaking out, Asher used the opportunity to grab the box of phones and hide it in plain sight on a shelf in the living room. He then quickly made his way to the family room, as that was where the group seemed to be convening.

Asher listened in as everyone discussed leaving and the locked gate, and then Lin asked the question on everyone's mind, "Where's the box with the phones?"

Asher used the opportunity to plant a false memory in everyone's mind, "It was a small brown box, and it was sitting right there." Asher said, knowing full well the box was black. Everyone was so frantic that no one questioned what Asher said, and now everyone was looking for the wrong colour box.

As everyone split up to look for the box or possibly a landline, Asher snuck into the kitchen and put a drop of cyanide into each of the water glasses sitting on the counter. He then joined the rest of the group in the parlour as they tried the phone.

"Did you turn it on, moron?" He said just to seem like he was as worried as everyone else and

205

knowing full well that there was no working landline in the house, he and Courtney had become quite friendly planning the surprise.

The group returned to the family room, and Asher got ready for the next part of his plan, time to kill Amy. He knew that Amy suffered from awful panic attacks and figured that she would start to lose it any time now. The water in the kitchen was already poisoned and ready to go; all he had to do was get someone to bring her a drink.

Right on cue, Amy started to panic, "Someone get her some water!" He yelled from the far side of the room, but just as Brook was about to get the water, the lights started to flicker. This isn't part of the plan, he thought to himself. Amy was standing right at the door, leaning on the doorframe, panicking. Asher had a sudden thought, change or plans.

As the lights continued to flicker, Asher nonchalantly picked up a stone statue from the table beside him. As soon as the lights were fully out, he took the chance and moved across the room to where Amy had been standing, trying his best to bump into as few people as possible.

Asher couldn't exactly see where he was going, but he did his best to hit Amy on the top of the head; she let out a blood-curdling scream. Asher grabbed Amy by the foot and dragged her from the family room to the living room. He hoped that by putting Amy's body in the same room as the phones, it would be less likely for the others to find them.

Once Asher had dumped Amy's body in the living room, he sprinted back to the family room and tried to join in on the shock and surprise. Not long after Asher returned to the family room, the lights came back on. Everyone was shocked by the trail of blood going down the hall, even Asher. He didn't realize Amy was bleeding that much when he dragged her down the hall. Asher looked down to check double he didn't have any blood on him, nothing that he could see.

Derek, of course, wanted to go look for Amy, and Asher seized the opportunity to go with him just in case Amy had somehow survived. He didn't want Derek to find her without him. What Asher didn't expect was for Layla to follow them.

Chapter 18
THE MURDERS, AGAIN

As Derek and Asher followed the blood, Asher made a point to step in the blood. He figured it was better to have a plausible reason he was tracking blood around the house in case it came to that. As Asher and Derek approached Amy's body, Layla appeared out of nowhere, "Who did this? Who? Amy! Amy!" She screamed as she rocked back and forth, holding Amy.

Asher and Derek eventually pulled Layla away from Amy and helped her to the doorway. Derek made a comment about not destroying evidence, and that was the exact thing Asher needed to hear. If everyone was worried about destroying evidence, then they wouldn't go in the room, and if they didn't go in the room, they wouldn't find the phones. Now, on to the next part of his plan to start getting rid of the rest of them. At the moment, Asher was the only one with a clear motive to kill Amy but no motive to kill the others. He knew if he wanted to avoid suspicion, Amy's death just wasn't enough.

Layla told the others what had happened and brought up the notes and the numbers; everything she was doing was working exactly into his plan; if he hadn't known better, he would have thought she was in on it. The group moved back to the dining room to reexamine the box when Colleen started to have a panic attack since she was number two.

Asher noticed Claire was walking around with one of the cups of water he'd poisoned. If she died next, it would ruin everything. Thankfully she put it down on the table before actually taking a sip. Michelle picked up the glass and handed it to Colleen, who took a big sip and was dead within a minute.

If everything had stopped there, Asher would have been happy. He had absolutely no connection to Colleen, and she was the least well-liked among the guests, which is why he'd chosen her to be second.

But he wanted more of them gone and hoped he could lead the others to unknowingly help with his plan.

Back in the family room, Derek started pushing everyone to read their notes, but Asher wanted to keep things moving, so he proposed that they split into groups, one to search for the phones and one to try and open the gate. Asher was glad that Derek was on board with the plan and was even happier when he suggested that Asher go with the group to check the gate.

Asher's group was the first out of the room, and on the way out, he made a point of having a quick word with Lin. "Lin, how are you? I didn't realize you and Anders knew Kara so well. Amy talked so much about each of you but never about you both together." Lin looked over and saw Anders and Kara talking closely. Asher continued walking on his way out of the house.

Once outside, Asher put the next part of his plan in motion. He pulled his car around and made sure he had the foaming candy in his pocket ready to go. As Asher and Jack tried to get over the gate, Asher made a point of seeming exhausted and winded.

"Michy, can you pass me my water bottle? It should be in the car." Asher said, getting ready to fake his own death.

Just as Asher took a swig of water, Brook and Bryce returned to share the news that they had found a small opening in the fence. Perfect timing. Asher put the Alka-seltzer in his mouth and chomped down hard to make sure that it foamed, then slumped down on the far side of his car, out of view from the house.

Everything that happened right after was a total coincidence, but it worked perfectly for Asher's plan. Derek and the inside group came out of the house to share the news that Lin had killed Anders just as the sky opened with rain forcing them to leave Asher's body where it was.

Once Asher was sure everyone was out of sight, he grabbed the guns out of the trunk and made his way to the back of the house. He slowly and quietly re-entered through the unlocked kitchen door. He stood silently in the kitchen for a moment, allowing himself to drip dry. He heard everyone head upstairs and close their doors.

Asher moved into the dining room to wait for everyone to make their next move. He was just about to head towards the stairs when he heard people start to come out of the bedrooms. Asher backed up and listened. "Let's head to the basement," Derek said as footsteps started to head downstairs.

Asher waited until he could no longer hear footsteps on the stairs, then began to sneak upstairs. When Asher got to the top of the stairs, he stopped in his tracks. Mick was sitting in the hall, playing with his phone. Asher couldn't believe his luck; Mick had kept his phone which meant he could still keep in touch with him. Asher quickly and quietly snuck into the closest bedroom and took his phone out of his pocket. 'Mick, I need you to do something for me.' Asher sent Mick a text and waited. No reply. Asher stuck his head out of the door, and Mick was asleep in the chair.

Asher walked carefully and quietly to the bedroom Lin was in, opened the door and stepped inside. She was asleep too; what was with these people? Asher moved quickly and quietly and found a blunt object to hit her over the head with. Lin's head drooped to the side almost instantly, and Asher got to work creating a noose out of the ropes holding the curtains open.

Lin came to just as Asher let go of her legs. She grabbed at her neck and gasped for air, then hung lifeless from the ceiling fan. Asher searched her pockets, found her note, changed her number to five and threw it on the ground. He then slowly opened the door, checking to see if Mick was still asleep; he was. Asher set the door to lock, pulled it closed behind him and made his way into the main bedroom at the end of the hall to wait.

It was a long time before the group came back upstairs, Asher wasn't sure what they'd been doing in the basement, but they seemed to be on a mission when they came back upstairs. Asher heard as they discovered Lin's body and then immediately accused Mick. More arguing and fighting, and then Mick's voice was the only one left, "Hey! Get your asses back up here and untie me! You can't leave me like this!"

Asher left the room he'd been hiding in and went to where Mick was being held. "What? Where the hell did you come from?" Mick said in complete shock to see Asher standing before him. "I need you to do something for me. "Asher said, picking up the same object he had hit Lin with. "Are you here to untie me? Well, hurry up!" Mick struggled with the ropes.

"No, I'm here to create some confusion." Asher hit Mick on the side of the head and watched him slump to the side. He then grabbed his note and crossed out the one in sixteen, turning his number to six. He then grabbed his phone and looked at it; the battery was almost dead, probably not enough power for anyone to make a call with, and Asher's texts were coming through as 'Boss.'

Asher needed to decide on a calculated risk. Did he leave the phone with Mick and keep texting it so the others would find it or take it with him? He decided to leave it and draw the others to it; he wanted to keep things moving. Asher locked and closed the door to the bedroom and went to the room across the hall to wait.

It took a while, but eventually, he heard footsteps; someone was coming upstairs. Asher hid in the closet just in case someone decided to come into the room. But they didn't. Asher heard them go into the room next to where Lin and Mick's bodies were. He sent Mick a text, Ding. Asher waited to see if anyone heard it. He sent another, Ding. Finally, movement. Asher listened as whoever had been in the room next door rushed into the room and found Mick and the phone; he sent one more text for good measure, Ding. The phone had to be pretty much

dead by now, especially if they were trying to open it
or use it.

Asher sent one more text but didn't hear any
dings; the phone was dead. Perfect. Asher stood
silently in the closet and listened as everyone
discussed Mick being the murderer and what to do
next. It took a few minutes, but eventually, the group
headed out again. Once it was quiet, Asher walked
over to the window and looked outside; the rain had
stopped, and they were probably going to discover
his body was gone any minute, time to move on to the
next part of his plan.

Asher watched outside to see the moment
when they discovered his body was missing, then
listened at the door to see what would happen next.
He heard footsteps run down the upstairs hall and
down the stairs before heading to a cacophony of
voices at the bottom of the stairs. He heard a door
close, and voices became muted, but he could hear
them more through the vent. Asher was just about to
leave when he heard a door slam; what was that? He
waited for a minute; then, when he didn't hear
anything else, he decided to continue with his plan.
Asher left the bedroom, slammed the door and ran
down the stairs and into the library.

Crash! Someone broke a vase in the next room. Asher only hoped that he was right and that Michelle would freak out once Asher was accused of being the murderer. The only question that remained was who would follow her out to calm her down. He had a feeling it would be Raegan because she was the next marked to die, and she probably figured the safest person to be with was the wife of the supposed murderer, who was already skipped over.

Asher's bet paid off as not a moment later, Michelle and Raegan entered the library with Michelle sobbing and Raegan comforting her. "Hello ladies, have a seat," Asher said, using a gun to guide them to two chairs across from each other.

"Asher? What's going on? Help!" Raegan yelled, but Asher pointed his gun at her. Do it again, and you're dead.

"What's going on? Why are you doing this?" Michelle asked as calmly and quietly as she could.

"I don't have time for that right now, but I have a proposition for you ladies. Whoever shoots the other will live; sound good?"

Asher walked over to the small table between the chairs and put a gun down.

"What? Why?" Michelle said through tears.

"I'm going to count to five; if neither of you chooses to shoot the other, I will shoot you both." Raegan and Michelle looked at each other through teary eyes and stood up, both looking at the gun on the table between them. Asher stood close beside them, gun drawn.

"five, four, three, two…."Before Asher could get to one, Michelle picked up the gun and shot Raegan, killing her and not a moment later, Asher shot Michelle killing her. Asher quickly put the gun in Raegan's hand and ran next door to the family room to wait.

Everyone ran into the room to see what happened, and Asher took that opportunity to enact the final part of his plan as he stepped into the doorway of the room to reveal himself.

Chapter 19

THE REVEAL

Derek was the first one to see him, "I knew it! I knew you were behind this." Derek said, looking at everyone to see their reaction. Asher walked further into the room as everyone backed up around him.

"I told them that I would let whoever shot the other one live. Guess they made their choice." Asher said, walking towards the two bodies.

"Why? Why did they need to die? Why are you killing everyone? Have you lost your mind?" Derek said, losing his cool. Asher bent down between the two bodies and grabbed the guns off the floor. Brook and Bryce exchanged a glance; why hadn't they grabbed the guns when they had the chance?

Asher placed one of the guns in his pocket and turned to face the group. He used the gun to move the group further into the room as he moved towards the one and only door out of the library. Once the group was standing where he wanted them, Asher took the gun he was still holding and shot Derek in the head.

Bang.

He was killed instantly.

"Oh my god!" Brook screamed as the rest of the group looked on in horror. "I've been wanting to do that all night," Asher said with a loud sigh as he walked over and gently kicked Derek's leg to confirm he was, in fact, dead. Satisfied that Derek wasn't going anywhere, Asher turned around to make his way back to the doorway.

"To answer your question, Derek, you can thank your late wife for all of this!" Asher reached the doorway and turned back around to see the group huddled together, terrified.

"Oh, sorry, Derek. Guess I should have answered your question before killing you; my mistake." Asher continued looking mighty smug. Asher grabbed a seat in the chair closest to the door.

"Sit, relax! I want to explain why I killed Amy. I mean, I know I look like the bad guy here, but I can assure you I am not." Asher said as the remaining guests took a seat to hear what he had to say because they didn't have a choice.

Just as Jack was about to sit down, he grabbed the lamp closest to him and made a run at Asher, hoping to catch him off guard.

Bang.

Asher shot him dead, sending him crumbling to the ground.

"Now that you know I will happily kill all of you, can you please sit still for a moment while I fix myself a drink?" Asher got up from his chair and walked over to the bar cart, and began mixing himself a drink. He placed the gun on the cart beside him so that he could use both hands.

As soon as the gun went down, Kara and Marco had the same idea and decided to make a lunge for the gun while he was distracted. Unfortunately, he wasn't distracted enough. Asher picked the gun up off the bar cart, turned and fired.

Bang.

Bang.

Kara and Marco both crumbled to the ground leaving only Claire, Brook, Bryce and Layla still alive.

"What a shame. I was hoping to have more of you to share my story with, but that isn't the case." Asher took a sip of the drink he had just poured for himself and made his way back to his chair to sit down and relax. He was the only one still left in the 70s attire from earlier that evening.

"Where to begin? Well, I believe I overheard Derek filling you in on this part, but can you believe that my parents left Amy 80% of their money? EIGHTY PERCENT. Can you believe it? And the 'fortune' they said they were leaving us was a lot less than I expected it to be, and I had been racking up debt for years, assuming my eventual inheritance would more than cover it." Asher pulled his note out of his pocket and showed it to the group.

"You are broke." He said, reading the note aloud. "So I contested the will, ensuring that she couldn't get her hands on that extra 30%, but I knew I wasn't going to win. You see, my best bet was to take out Amy to get the money. My money. The money I was promised. The money I'd already spent. And I mean, I couldn't risk any of you ratting me out to the police, now could I." Asher looked around the room at all of the terrified faces.

"I don't understand why you bothered getting all those secrets about us," Bryce said, looking down at Derek's lifeless body. "Simple, it was a red herring. You were all so busy worrying about who knew your secrets that it took your attention, and the motive, off of me. Pretty smart, right?!"

Asher was so busy pontificating about why he was so smart that he didn't realize someone else had entered the room. He was just about to turn around and see who was standing behind him when Bryce asked another question to keep his attention.

"How did you find all of those secrets out? I mean, those were things that no one knew about."

Bryce took a deep breath, hoping he caught his attention in time; luckily, he did.

"Oh, come on, there's always a way to find out...." Before Asher could finish his thought, Mick hit him on the back of the head with a statue of a bear, knocking him to the ground.

"He hired me," Mick said, dropping the statue on the floor.

Claire ran over and wrapped Mick in a huge hug before letting go, suddenly feeling a little uncomfortable.

"What do you mean he hired you? You were working together this entire time?" Claire took a step back and stood with Layla, Brook and Bryce, the only other surviving members of the evening.

Mick stepped over Asher's unconscious body walking towards the others, which in turn took another step back.

"I'm a P.I. Asher paid me to investigate all of you, but he didn't pay me to be an accessory to murder," Mick said as Claire started to tense her shoulders. Suddenly, Asher started to move, and

Brook and Bryce jumped into action. They quickly grabbed some cords and used them to tie Asher's arms and legs while also ensuring he no longer had his gun.

"I don't get it. Were you using me? I'm so confused!" Claire said as she started to tear up talking to Mick.

"Believe it or not, I wasn't. We actually started dating before I was hired to look into all of you. Sorry I didn't tell you sooner, but my job depends on discretion. Mick said, putting a hand on Claire's shoulder.

"I can't believe I believed you were a plumber!" She said, starting to soften up, "I'm just glad you're ok" Claire and Mick hugged; she really was relieved that he was ok.

Brook wasn't feeling quite as charitable towards Mick and his lies. "Whoa, whoa, whoa. Mick, you're telling us you just sat there and watched people being murdered! Why didn't you say something? You could have stopped all of this with a single phone call. I mean, you had your phone with you the entire time." Brook said, starting to cry.

"I didn't know Asher was the murderer. I just called him Boss; he hired me anonymously. My phone also didn't have cell service in this house, I was on the wifi, but I couldn't make calls; I'm telling you, I wasn't in on his plan." Mick said, rooting around in Asher's pocket, looking for his phone.

"Asher was on the list of people to investigate. I investigated him just like I did all of you." Mick pulled out Asher's phone and used the emergency function to call 911.

"911, what's your emergency?" The 911 operator asked, answering the phone.

"I'm calling from 452 Walker Lane, Coldwater; it's a huge house behind a locked gate in the middle of the woods. There has been a series of murders, and we are trapped in the house; we have the killer retrained." Mick was very calm and collected while speaking to the 911 operator.

"Ok, stay put. Help is on the way." The operator said, ending the call.

"Cops are on their way," Mick said, hanging up the phone. The group shared a collective sigh of relief; the nightmare was finally over. We should wait in the parlour; it's the only room that isn't a crime scene. Mick, Bryce and Claire made their way out of the room while Brook stayed back.

Brook walked over to Layla and put a hand on her shoulder; she was still sitting on the ground with her arms around Raegan.

"We should go." She said to her gently. Layla barely even heard Brook's words, "Layla. Come on." Brook grabbed Layla's hand and finally got her attention.

"I. I can't. This is all my fault." Layla said to Brook, tearing up. Brook helped Layla up, "Nothing that happened tonight was your fault." Brook gave Layla a hug; she squeezed her back.

Brook and Layla walked out of the library just as Asher started to stir.

Chapter 20
THE TWIST

The survivors sat in the parlour staring into space; they were will numb from everything that had happened in the past few hours. The sun was just starting to come up; Bryce looked at the clock, 6:00 AM; how was it the next morning already? Mick started going through Asher's phone. He looked at their text change and couldn't help but cringe. Was all of this his fault? He then looked through his contacts and had an idea.

"We should text the other phones; if any of them are on, it will lead us to where the box was hidden."

Mick sent a text to Michelle's phone from Asher's phone.

Ding.

"I heard it! Did you hear that?" Brook asked, popping up.

"Send another one." Mick sent another phone, ding.

"I think it's coming from across the hall," Brook said, stepping out of the parlour.

"The cops are here!" Layla shouted, looking out the window. Suddenly, the phones didn't seem as important. The group rushed out the front door, where they saw the police on the other side of the gate.

"Are you the one who called us? Can you open the gate?" The police officer said, getting out of her car.

"No, we don't have the code," Brook said, realizing they really did need to find the phones. Layla turned her back to the group and very discreetly took her phone out of her pocket and texted, 'it's over.' There was a momentary pause, and then she got a reply, 'I'm coming out. I love you.'. Layla put her phone away, but Claire had seen everything that had gone on.

"What are we looking at here? How many bodies?" The second police officer asked. As another set of cops started examining the gate to see if they could figure out how to get in.

Layla piped in to answer, "Derek, Marco, Kara, Jack, Raegan and Michelle were all shot and are in the library. Anders was stabbed in the family room. Colleen was poisoned in the dining room, and Lin was hung upstairs. Nine bodies altogether, and Asher, the murderer, is tied up in the library." Layla said as the police officer wrote down the gruesome details.

"Ten, there are ten bodies; how could you forget Amy?" Brook said, starting to cry.

Before Layla could reply, the police officer cut in, "Who's that?" He asked, pointing to the person coming their way while also drawing his gun. The group turned around to see Amy walking towards them. "I have the code for the fence," Amy said as she made her way toward the gate. She looked hurt but very much alive.

"Amy!" Layla ran over and gave Amy a big hug; she hugged her back. Amy finished the walk to the gate and put the code in. The group backed up to allow the gate to open and to give room for the police and ambulance to drive in.

The cops quickly got out of their cars and made their way into the house while the friends headed to the ambulance to be checked out.

"Start with Amy; she was badly hurt; we thought she was dead!" Brook said, helping Amy towards the ambulance.

"Amy, what happened? You were dead! How are you alive? It was like ten hours ago when you died, or we thought you died." Brook said, wracking her brain to try and put together what was going on.

"Brook, take a breath; give her a minute," Bryce said, putting a hand on Brook's shoulder.

"It's ok; I owe you an explanation," Amy said as the paramedics took her blood pressure and put a blanket over her shoulders.

"When I opened the note, I panicked. I immediately knew that Asher was behind it, but before I could do anything, I was knocked out cold," Amy started tearing up, "to the point that everyone thought I was dead." Amy began to cry in Layla's arms, Bryce pulled Brook away, but she didn't feel right about the whole situation; something was up.

"Well, Amy, you seem to be fine. In fact, I'm not able to locate any wounds or skin abrasions. You have a bit of a bump, but certainly nothing serious and nothing that would have caused you to be unconscious for an extended period of time." The paramedic said while removing the blood pressure monitor.

As the paramedic walked away, Amy leaned into Layla, "Well, that was easier than I thought it would be." Layla smiled at her, "How did you know Asher was going to go crazy and murder everyone?" Layla was trying her best to keep her voice down.

"Michelle and I had been messaging back and forth; I knew how upset Asher was about the money and how much he wanted to be invited to my party. I figured he was going to try and kill me so I hid some fake blood in my bra in case I needed to convince him I was dead. Then when the lights went out, it was perfect; Asher hit me, but as you saw, not nearly hard enough to kill me, and when he dragged me down the hall, the fake blood got everywhere; I didn't even have to do anything." Amy took Layla's hand.

"I was so glad you were the one who came to me so I could let you know I was all right. And the fact that he killed Derek and Raegan as well, perfect." Amy might not have been the murderer, but it was becoming increasingly clear that she wasn't a victim either.

"And when you came to check on me, and I could give you your phone, so we could stay in touch, it made me feel so much better. Good thing Asher hid the box of phones in the room with me." Amy said, leaning into Layla's shoulder.

As Amy and Layla sat together, Asher was brought out of the house by the police. As he was escorted down the driveway, he was almost in a trance, like he was no longer connected to his body, that is, until he saw Amy.

"What? No! You're dead! You're dead! I killed you; I killed you first!" Asher broke free from the police and raced towards Amy. He was just about to get to her when Layla got in the way.

Asher shoved Layla to the ground hard, where she hit her head on the driveway. Thankfully Layla slowed Asher down enough that the cops could restrain him.

"She was dead. I killed her. She was dead." Asher continued to mumble to himself all the way to the police car. The cops put him inside and drove away; the nightmare was finally over.

Amy was cradling Layla when the cops came over and moved her away. Layla had a nasty head wound and needed medical attention. As Amy moved away, Brook came over to chat with her. "So, do you want to tell me what's going on?" Brook asked, looking her best friend in the eye.

"Other than the fact my brother went crazy and murdered my husband and half my friends," Amy said, trying to play on Brook's sympathy, but Brook wasn't having it.

"Ya, other than that," Brook said, starting to get a lump in her throat. Amy was only half listening to Brook and seemed to be more concerned with what was happening with Layla than anything Brook was saying.

"Just go," Brook said, releasing Amy from the conversation.

"Amy!" Brook called as Amy turned around. "Just promise me you had nothing to do with this." Amy blew Brook a kiss and then went to sit beside Layla. Brook looked down and saw Amy's phone sitting on the ground beside her. She reached down and picked it up, and suddenly the truth slapped her in the face.

Amy could have stopped this at any time but didn't. The paramedics checked her out, and she was barely injured; there is no way she was unconscious for like 10 hours and then magically woke up as soon as the police arrived. She had her phone the entire time; she could have called for help or unlocked the gate at any point.

Amy knew Asher was killing people, and she did nothing to stop it. She wanted Derek dead. She wanted Raegan dead. Amy might not have been the murderer, but she was just as much to blame for everyone's death. She knew who the murderer was, and she could have stopped it at any point.

Amy looked over to Brook, and Brook waved, holding Amy's phone, which got her attention.

"Be right back," Amy said to Layla as she jogged over to get her phone from Brook.

"Thanks." She said, grabbing the phone from Brook's hand. Amy turned to walk away, but Brook wasn't done with her yet.

"So, you had your phone the entire time." Amy turned to face Brook but said nothing. Brook continued. "With the code for the gate and the ability to call for help." Amy continued staring at her silently. "You could have stopped this. You could have stopped people from dying. You could have stopped your friends from dying." Amy silently stepped closer to Brooke, sending a chill down her spine.

Brook took a deep breath; she wasn't backing down. "Why didn't you stop it?" Brook said, looking Amy straight in the eye. Amy took another step closer.

"Because if I stopped it, I wouldn't have gotten what I wanted." Amy turned and walked away, leaving Brook shaken and confused.

"You ok?" Bryce asked, walking over and putting an arm around Brook. Brook looked to Amy and then to Bryce, "Yeah, I think so." Bryce and Brook walked away, and Brook felt as though her best friend was still dead even though she was very much alive.

Bryce and Brook joined Mick and Claire on the far side of the driveway, leaving Layla and Amy alone. "Look," Mick said, nodding his head in the direction of the house. The others turned to see the bodies of their friends being brought out of the house; it was gruesome.

While everyone looked at the bodies going by, Brook had her eyes on Layla and Amy, something had changed in the last few minutes, and she was curious to know what it was.

"So what do we do now?" Layla said, leaning on Amy.

Amy shifted away from her slightly. "It's probably best we don't see each other for a while. We

236

don't want people to get suspicious." Amy said in a suddenly icy tone.

Layla was confused and upset, "Suspicious? Suspicious of what? We didn't do anything wrong. Asher did." Layla was starting to feel panicked.

"He sure did, but what if he had an accomplice? What if someone knew what was going on and did nothing to try and stop it? What if someone covered up that they knew someone wasn't really dead in order to keep the murders going? What if someone wanted someone dead and let other innocent people die so that that person would be killed without them lifting a finger? What if someone else was just as guilty as Asher?" All of the colour drained from Layla's face; what was happening?!

"What? What are you saying? I don't understand!" Layla was almost in tears now. "I'm not saying anything. Just looking at some hypothetical situations where someone else might also be guilty, that's all." Amy was getting smug now.

Mick walked away from the group and over to Amy and Layla; he could tell by their body language that something more was going on.

"You ladies doing ok?" He asked, approaching the two of them.

"Yeah, we're fine. Thanks." Amy replied with a 'keep your nose out of it' tone.

"That's good because, from a distance, it looked like you were fighting. It almost looked like you had a plan that maybe wasn't working out quite as well as you thought it would. Like Layla knew all along that Amy wasn't dead and that both of you had your phones with you and didn't call the police for help, even though you actually had service out here in the middle of nowhere." Mick stopped talking and stared at the two of them for a moment, "But what do I know? I mean, I'm new here." Mick started to walk away before turning and looking at Layla. "How did you know there were only nine bodies before Amy came out of the house?"

"What are you talking about? I listed Amy when I told the cops about who had died." Layla said defensively.

"Did you? I could've sworn you didn't include her. My mistake." Mick starts to walk away again, but Amy stopped him.

"Hey!" Mick turned back to face Amy.

"What do you want?" She asked.

"What makes you think I want something?" Mick said with a half-smile.

"If you weren't trying to blackmail us, you would have just gone to the police and told them what you know or what you think you know, but instead, you came to us. So, what do you want?" Amy was getting angry.

"You know what, you're right; I'm so glad you asked. I want money and lots of it." Mick said with a smirk.

"How much?" Amy asked. "80% of your inheritance, and I know you're getting the full amount now." Mick wasn't playing games anymore.

"Are you kidding me? No way!" Amy said so loudly that she got the attention of the others.

"Ok, your choice. Thanks for the good idea of talking to the police; I think I might do that instead, clear my conscious." Mick started to walk away, but this time it was Layla that got his attention.

"She'll do it. She'll give you the 80%." Layla said suddenly.

"Like hell I will! This isn't your money to give away." Amy said, pulling even further away from Layla.

"Maybe not, but I'm going to be the one going to jail if you don't give the money to Mick," Layla said in full-on panic mode.

Amy was quiet for a moment then a smile came across her face.

"You're right. Mick, screw you. Tell the police what you know. Layla, you're on your own." Amy turned to walk away, and Layla couldn't take it anymore. She bent down, picked up the closest rock she could find and bashed Amy across the head, hard. Amy crumbled to the ground; there was no question she was dead this time.

All of the commotion had gotten the attention of the cops, who came running over. "I witnessed everything. Layla snapped and hit Amy over the head with a rock."

As the cops dragged Layla away from Amy's lifeless body, she couldn't stop crying, "Nooooo. Amy, I love you."

Brook, Claire and Bryce ran over, shocked. No one could believe what had happened. "Oh my god, what just happened?" Brook asked, sobbing.

"Layla snapped and hit Amy over the head with a rock; she's definitely dead this time. I think she felt guilty since she was an accomplice to the murders. They both were." Mick said, walking over to Claire.

"What do you mean? They were involved, I can't…I mean, I wondered…But no. There's no way." Brook was having a hard time processing the idea that Amy really wasn't the person she thought she was.

"This is all so crazy. I wonder what will happen to the inheritance now; this has to be pretty irregular." Bryce said as the paramedics covered Amy's body with a blanket.

"Easy. It goes to the next living relative, their only cousin. I looked into the details of the will when I was researching everyone. Once I started to learn about all of you, I had a feeling the death of Amy and

Asher's parents somehow played into what was going on." Mick said, kissing Claire on the cheek.

"Wait a minute? Their only cousin, that's…." Brook looked at Claire, who was already smiling.

"Me. Guess I'm walking away from this weekend 10 million dollars richer." Claire said with a smile.

"Did you, did you know?" Brook asked, her head spinning with all of the deceptions. Was everyone in on this? Were she and Bryce the only ones who didn't have an ulterior motive?

"Let's go; we need to pay a visit to the lawyer," Claire said, grabbing Mick's hand. The two of them went over and talked to the police officer for a second before getting in their car and driving away.

Brook and Bryce stared at each other for a long moment before Brook finally said what they were both thinking, "What the hell just happened here?"

THE END

COMING SOON
BOOK TWO: A FAMILY AFFAIR

Family reunions can be murder.

It was the summer of 1995 when the Abbot family was finally ready to have the family reunion they had been organizing for nearly two years. Siblings, cousins, parents, grandparents, relatives were flying in from all over North America to take part in the once-in-a-generation family festivities. There were 40 people in total, all staying in cottages on a remote island in Northern Ontario that is only accessible by boat. The weekend starts off well enough but quickly goes downhill when old quarrels are brought up, and new secrets are revealed. The family is practically ready to call the reunion quits when a storm rolls in, stranding them on the island.

As soon as they realize that there is no leaving the island, all hell breaks loose, literally, as family members begin dropping like flies. Can the remaining family work out which of them is behind the murders before it's too late? Or is it just a matter of time before all of them are dead, but one?

Scan the QR Code below to see S.A.'s full collection as well as exclusive short mysteries.

mysteryandsuspense.ca

Be sure to join the mailing list for new release information and more!

ABOUT THE AUTHOR

S. A. Warren has been a professional writer for almost twenty years and is very excited to see her debut novel, Body Count, come to life. S.A. has always been a big fan of thrillers, mystery and horror and is excited to infuse her passion into her new book series.

Be sure to keep an eye out for the next book in the Someone's Always Lying series- A Family Affair.

www.ingramcontent.com/pod-product-compliance
Lightning Source LLC
Chambersburg PA
CBHW011150190726
48288CB00010B/3259